CONNECTIONS 2

Example page

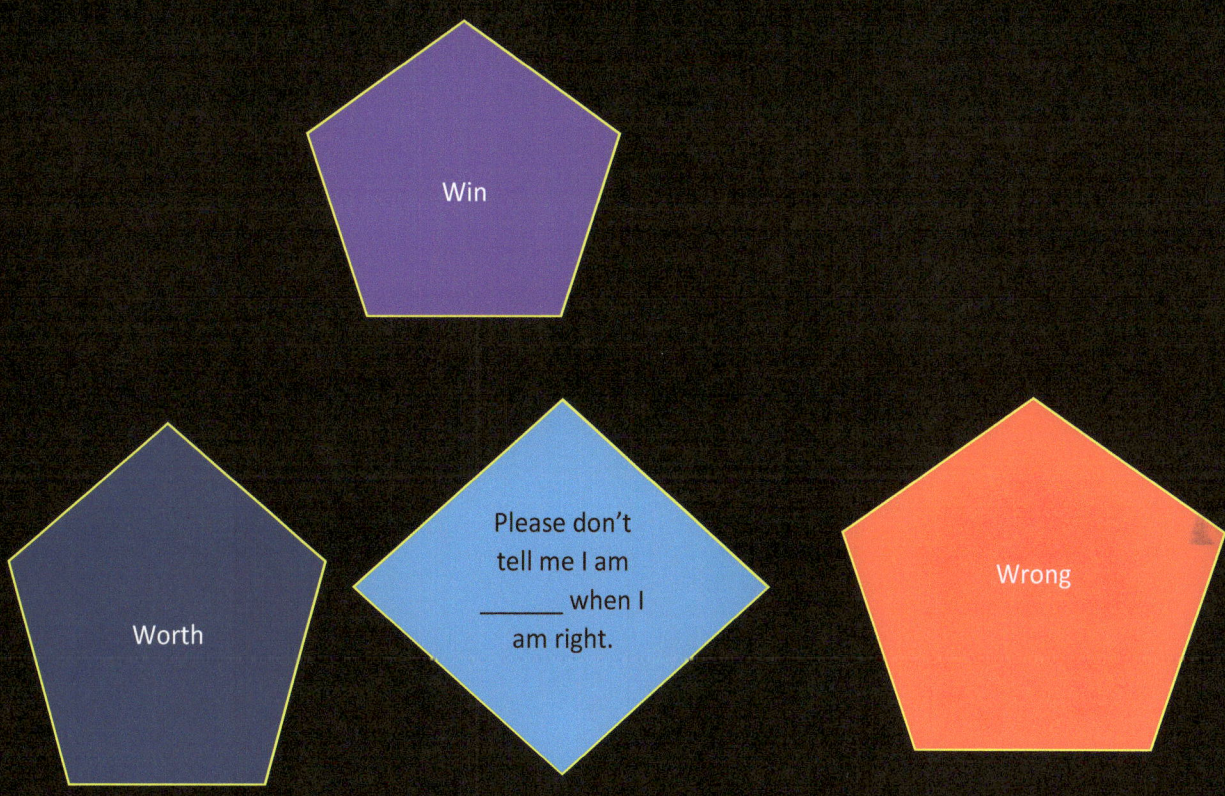

Fill in the blanks with the best word choices.
Sometimes the same word will be used more than once.

Enjoy the words, phrases, and sentences that decorate the page.
Hang on to your seats!

Connections 2
By Roshinaie Johnson

1.

Eye transference in robots.
 Voice transference.

All of this life thus far to wake up to this.

QUARTERS

Perfect timing: Arrival. Birth.

PENNIES

DIMES

The bottom line is these people were good for nothing.

CENTS

SCENT

SENT

SINCE

SENSES

They want a second chance above ground.

Robots.
                All eyes in computer and live.
The Way Out.
                How everything was made.
Locations everything was made.
The Money.

Time frame it will take to get them out.
How bodies injected with the device.

                Drill it in. 3 times a day I need to watch footage.
                Mandatory.

The dance team competition.

2.

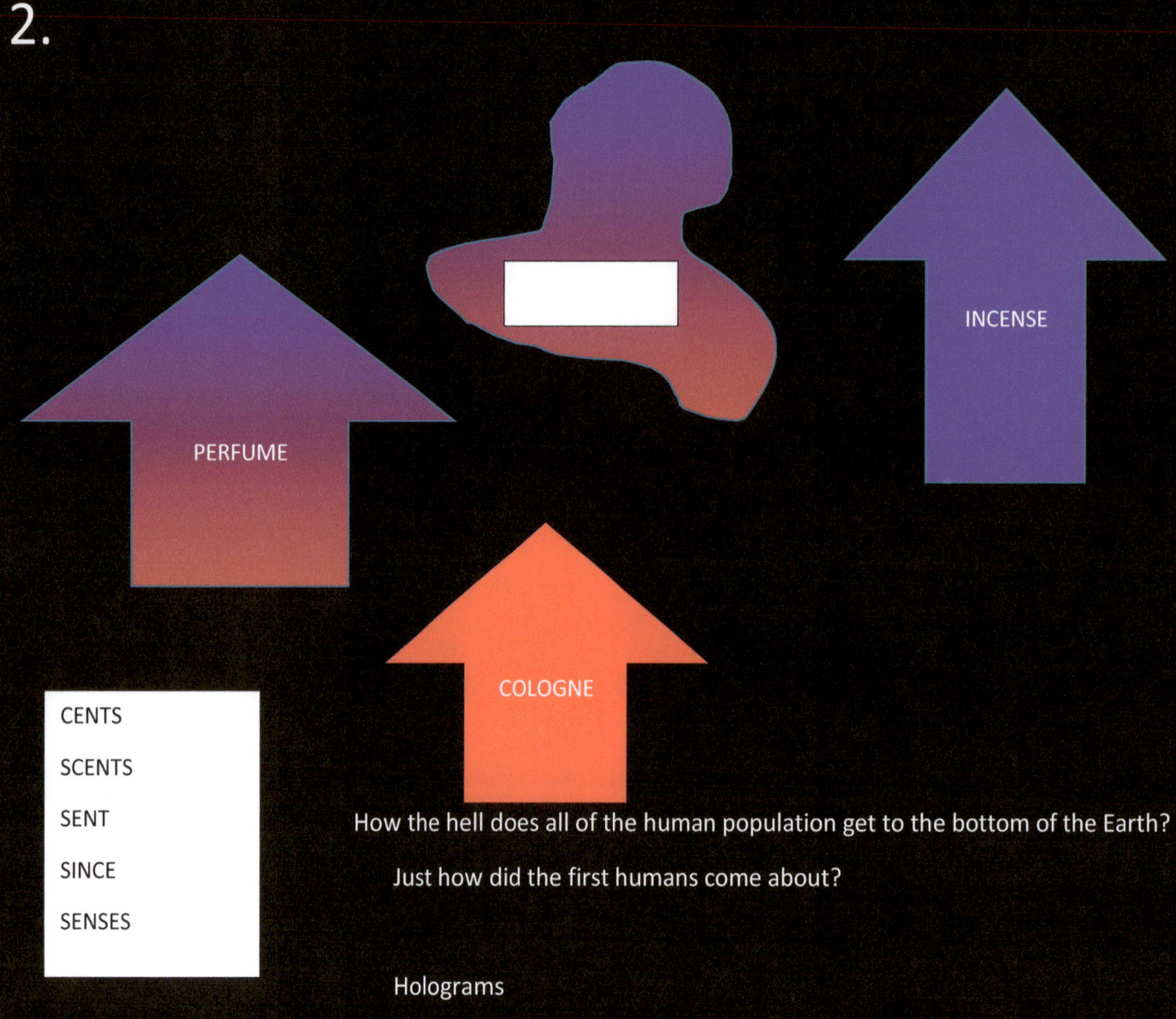

PERFUME

INCENSE

COLOGNE

CENTS

SCENTS

SENT

SINCE

SENSES

How the hell does all of the human population get to the bottom of the Earth?

Just how did the first humans come about?

Holograms

If my way, when water appeared in the clip, water would sprinkle out.

Quick. Had to disperse/separate family.
Some of my siblings were already grown and living on their own.

The clamp to the underground.

What are they doing? Killing, cleaning. Trying to inch their way forward. Back and forth they go.
Chemicals that kill shit. Make it vanish. Devices that suck shit up since at rock bottom there's nowhere for it to go.

Revelations to the world.

3.

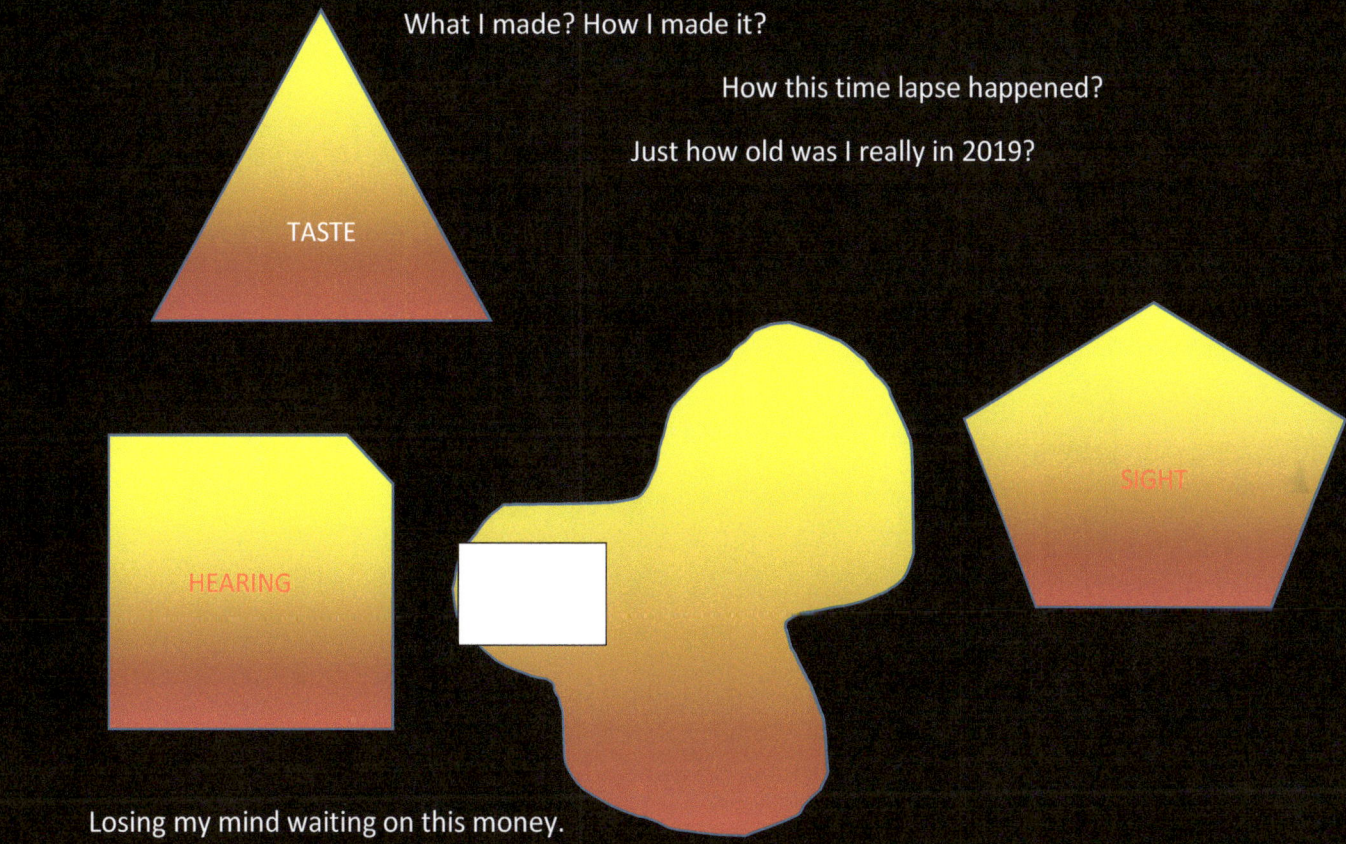

What I made? How I made it?

How this time lapse happened?

Just how old was I really in 2019?

TASTE

SIGHT

HEARING

CENTS

SCENT

SENT

SINCE

SENSES

Losing my mind waiting on this money.

Every time I hear about money. Every time I see real or fake money.
I want to go insane.

The thought of paying off debt. Buying groceries. Buying a house.
All the things they wish to do when they are free.

My family and I could be locked in a cage. At rock bottom, if it weren't for my skill set.
With the rest of the population.

Dealing with trances. Brain shut downs. People turning into criminals. Nasty smells. Eating poop, shit, and dead
bodies. Animals included. Eating grass, dirt. Drinking blood. Animal secretions.

4.

A. I _____ him to the store.

B. On Christmas he wants a pre_____.

C. He _____ the bad girl away.

CENTS
SCENT
SENT
SINCE
SENSES

Don't need to go anywhere.

Stay busy.

There are some good beasts down there helping them.
They're going for them to get out.

They can't kill the beasts because they need them to kill the shit monsters and keep electronic human creations from hurting or killing them.
They have alliances.

Interviews.
They sit down there and talk about them.
No drugs.
Everyone at rock bottom.
We'd all be dead.
Perfect arrival.
Secret places to send things.
The point. So they can feel and smell the air up here.
Storage, backpack, wallet, prepaid cards. All things I plan to get when I get some money.

Sight, taste, smell, touch, hearing.
Inventions, injections, things to keep people alive that are never heard of. Will never be heard of. The creators, never revealed.

A. _____ you don't like me, I'll go home.

B. He went to a restaurant _____ you didn't cook.

C. He's taking a long time _____ you did yesterday.

CENTS

SCENT

SENT

SINCE

SENSES

I'm ten years old. I think. My birthday, the real one, is August 29th or December 25th. The year. I can't think of it right now. I have over 25 brothers. This is not my real family.

Real Ghost Stories. With Real People.
Keep up!   Brothers!   Mommy!   Me!

Debt: taxes, eviction, general relief, cable, electricity, water, court, gas company.
One of these companies owes me some money.

My bank account. I can't get one at a particular one anymore. Bad checks by a dumb and evil fine ass boy. He tricked the damn machine.
What the fuck was I thinking letting him give me a check. I realized what he did later. Oh well.

A. Which of these is a color?

```
READY

READ

RED
```

B. He _____ the book out loud.

```
READY

READ

RED
```

C. Are you _____ to go?

```
READY

READ

RED
```

These people have us fucked up.
These are my siblings and we scattered.

I have no idea exactly how many of us there are.

The mind has to be read to figure out how to get them out. No.

To let them know what happened to them.

At times they seem to have complete trust that whenever I come is best.

Now the slaves are figuring out what their ancestors set them up for. Why they kill other countries people.

Now they're even madder.

They're popping up in areas of other people that need a lot of help.

Not right. Easily locatable. Humans. Jobs get all of our information.

7.   Complete army above. Bullets given. Weight. Heat. Wind.

Need credit company to help clear my credit report so I can get another account.
$595

BALLOON

BUBBLE GUM

BUBBLES

WHAT CAN YOU DO TO THESE
THREE THINGS?

   A.   BLUE
   B.   BLOW

These people are grown as fuck.   Mommy!

These people will come above ground and fuck everything up.
I created an army.
Then I would've made these videos for nothing.
People become enemies and then in danger.

The story: what happened here?
The truth.
Since day one of mankind.

They're naked.

Which is a color?

BLUE

BLEW

Some of these people, the rotten ones, thought and still think they will get out alone and take o

The wind _____ the
leaves in front of his
yard.

BLOW

BLUE

BLEW

Some people kept having kids in hopes that someone would change everything.
With no account, invest in myself.
Will reunite with family.
Will walk back into labs.
Will create more things.

Celebrity. Celibate. Britty. Pretty names chosen.
New email.

Mistakes in the first documents. That table is coming back. The ones

they ate at when they came up with bullshit ways for people to talk.

Starting to feel the youthfulness in me. Brain shots.

They can taste the freedom.
Said these were my soul mates. #1's. Numero Unos. I'm no hoe like most of them.

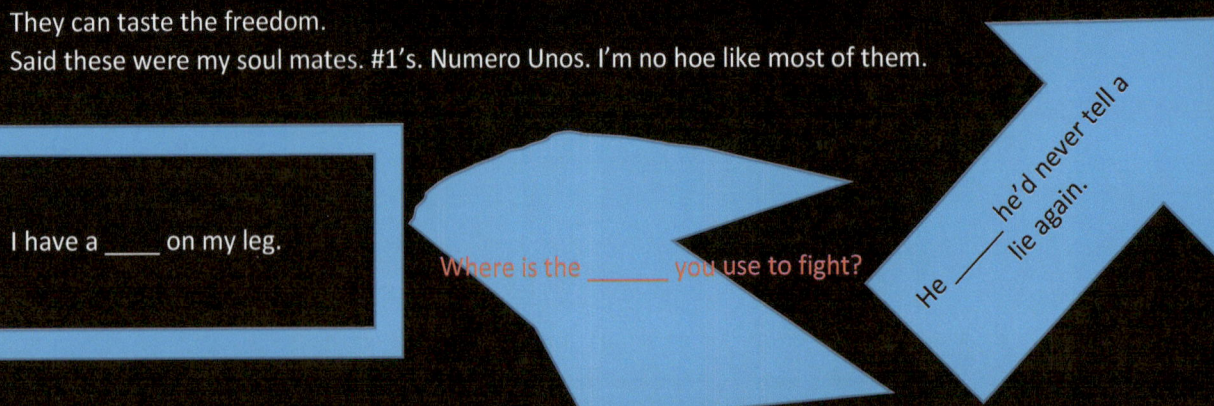

Soar

Sore

Sword

Swore

I have a _____ on my leg.

Where is the _____ you use to fight?

He _____ he'd never tell a lie again.

Fill in the blanks with one of the words in the box above.

They want to know what the sex was like while they were tortured.
They want to know everything.

Music. They sing live. Did they learn why people trashed them when others had trances?
How many times am I showing up? Once.
They are estimating how much shit is being taken out.
The dream. The room. Downstairs location. A man giving snacks to inmates.
They all have faith (hope and faith) to get out regardless of what they're being taught. Hit them in the head. Ball in sock.
Storage location.
Stuck down there: up and down phases.
I said they were sensitive.
Cameras down there recording them and making more videos. Or is it just the animals still scaring them?

Talking beasts? Well there's talking robots.

Books. Work contacts.

I can feel the blood moving in my head with the headaches from these people. It's like scabs are being formed. Sores in my brain. My fucking head.

I have to keep in mind that these people are in pain constantly. Constantly being tortured by beasts.

Small things like, knowing I have to do creations in this book, and knowing I will have to save it again to my email so I may/might as well type this sentence and other ones I think of every time I add knew things to it, that don't come naturally because I have met such mean people fucking with me or, pure idiots.

That one mean girl at the restaurant, fucking up my brain.

People don't talk about it because, the beast. They don't talk about the crazy things they've seen to friends because they think they'll sound stupid or society somehow has naturally made it feel weird to say such things, or you to feel dumb, or you think your friend will think you're dumb. How they do that?

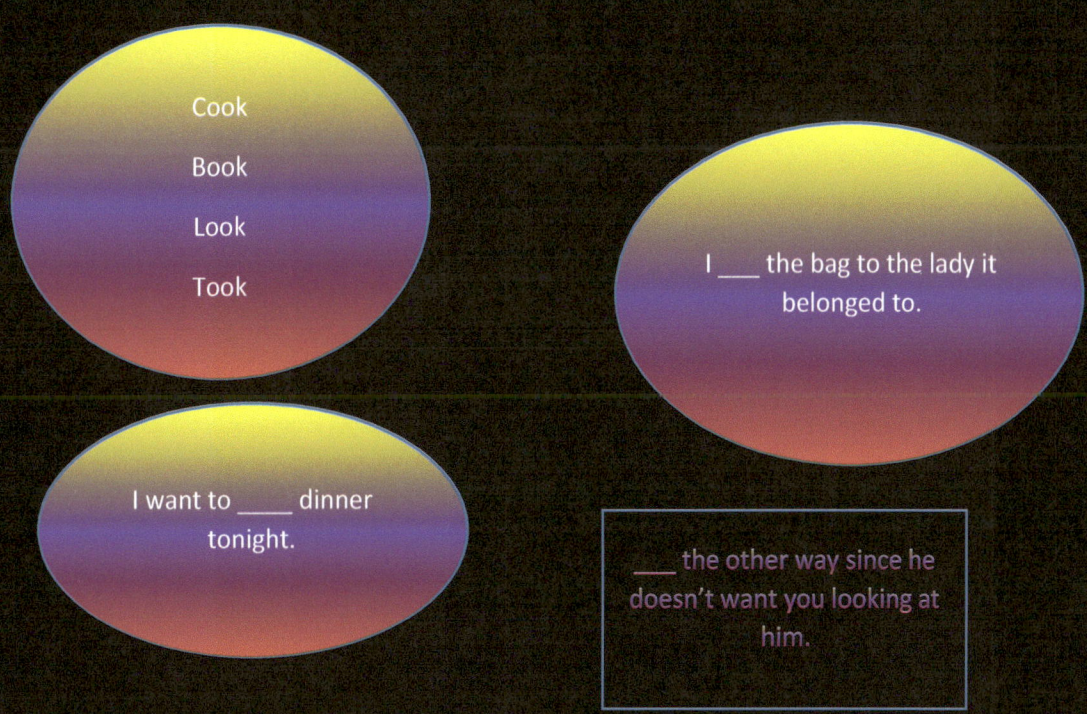

Need to go to various different places.

Need a clamp. Not guess.

Done. Something's happened with me, nature, God to let me know that these people are breathing or not.

Real. How can I judge how these people will view me when I never experienced them?
Discipline and Trust.
Discipline & Trust.

Just think of ways to get even on the spot. Would I make a robot lie to me to stay alive?
Don't take evil from people out on other people. Take it out on the same evil people and quick. The odds you'll see them again. Uh oh. These visions. Random people your mind created snapping on the air, people you're mad at or another made up person.

There's no way to know all this information.
Things will play out in front of me.

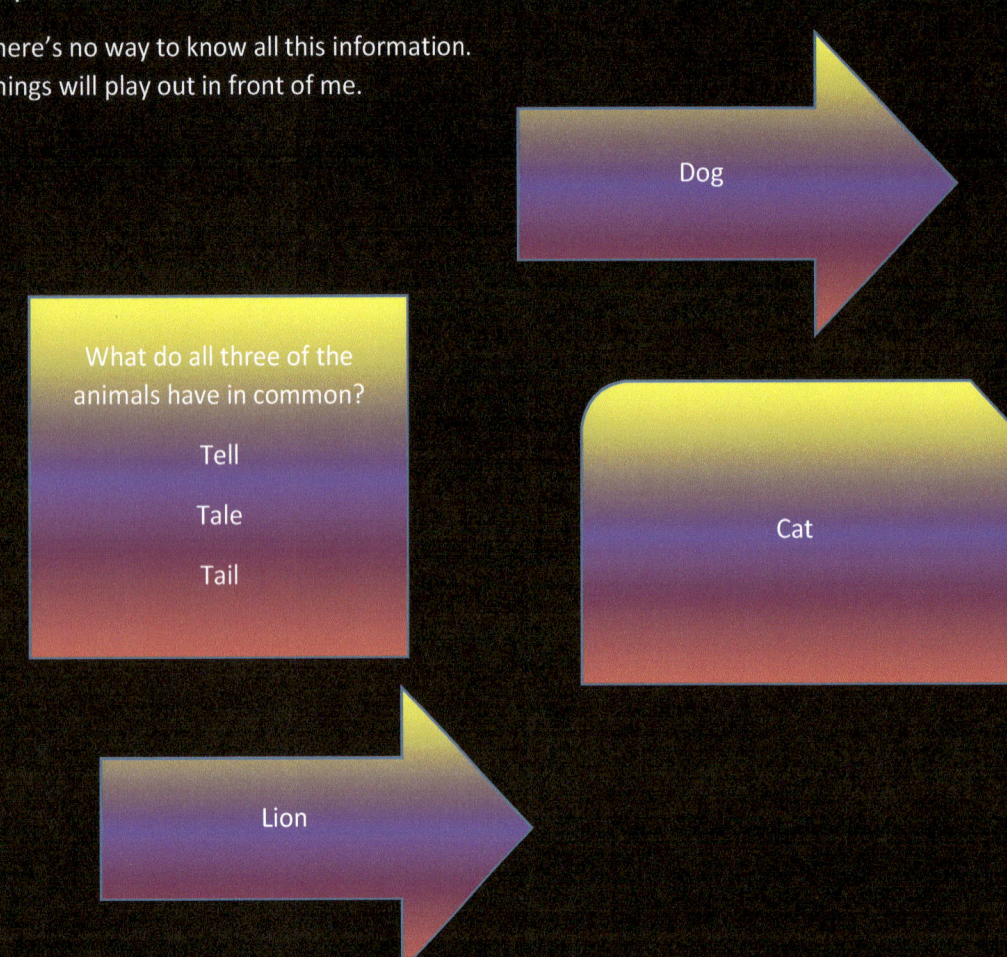

Dog

What do all three of the animals have in common?

Tell

Tale

Tail

Cat

Lion

Uh oh. Momma can feel my growth. And that I'm getting near to her. Lady next to me smells like that good stuff.

Trust – my younger self would not tease my older self about money.
If I'm waiting, it's for a reason and more I need to learn.
I mean it. I'm not trying to kill myself.

Shouldn't care no way if anyone likes me. That statement goes with another statement I made prior. People making others suicidal.

This is a dangerous game we play.

The song just snapped me out of suicide later. That shit there.

Supposed to watch my family.

Thoughts swiped.

These things can transform into anything and make you smell anything. All of this for nothing? Nope. These people are alive
I need to stick to the schedule when I clamp it in.

Everything's written.

Sexy typing to songs.

The events will piece together from whatever's there already written.

The song. The voice.

The voices of these people implanted and. So they can sing live but the drastic change can't be to.
Wait. The voices of these people so they can sing live and I don't have a heart attack if they hit the notes different.

Show things.
When is enough, Enough?

Human characteristics. Suicide feel. God would have told his child, no one else was around. Need to make robots. He can make anything. Could've made another creation before putting his child here.

There's a new meaning to page bleed.

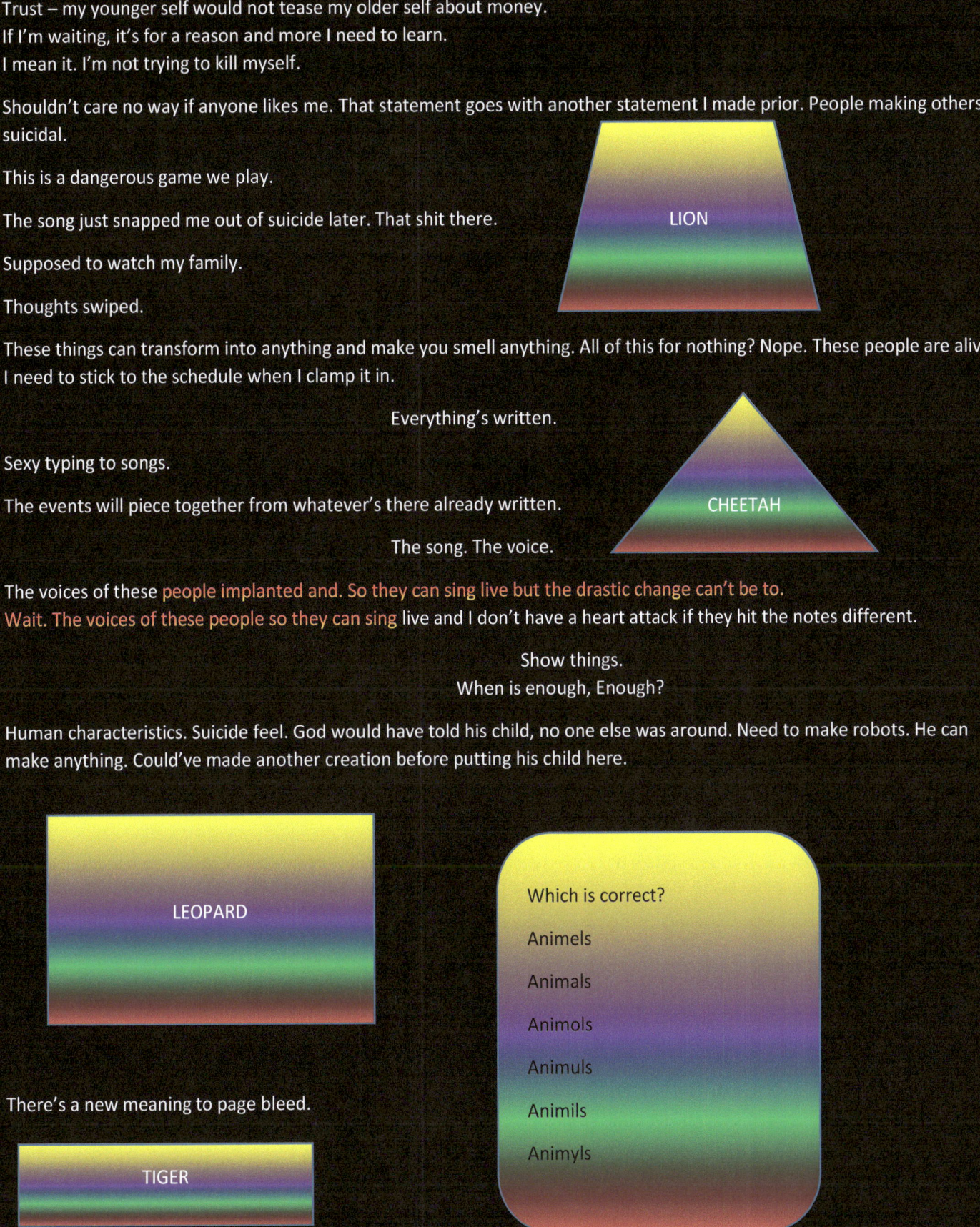

LION

CHEETAH

LEOPARD

TIGER

Which is correct?

Animels

Animals

Animols

Animuls

Animils

Animyls

The song played just on time. The right lyrics to keep me afloat. I could've created a brilliant being, robotic or whatever instead of giving things to the deceased.

Decorations.

Mommy's 10 year old baby. Or am I 9 or 8? I'm big as hell.

Pure hell.

No way to talk with your face and gestures.
I said they were in their cages acting out the scenes.

Their masters weren't letting them out and hopping in their bodies. The animals think they are them.

I mean it. It's all in here.

BERRY
BURY
VERY
VARIES
VARIOUS

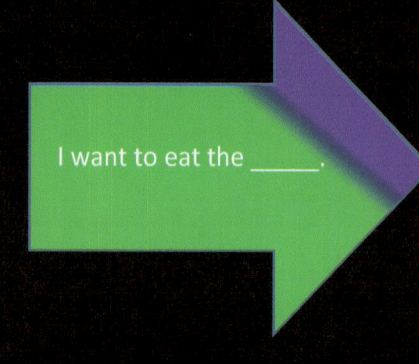

I want to eat the _____.

Suicide walks in and out. One robot walks in – a good sign one robot walks out gives me a bad vibe.

And then there were what?
Discipline and Trust.

This type of mind reading to fuck with you.

Book Discipline.

It's a dangerous game we play. Suicide the outing factor. You have it all the way or it inserts in you depending on where you land or what you see, then it leaves, no it stays completely when you exit the game.

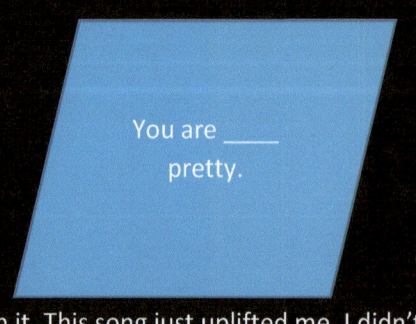

You are _____ pretty.

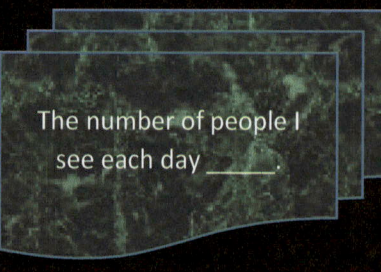

The number of people I see each day _____.

I mean it. This song just uplifted me. I didn't choose it. I chose the prior one and this one was automatically up next. This type of shit to fuck with you.

They left nothing here and all hell is what they shall get in return.

Robot facial changes messing with your forehead and body feel.

We can't believe this shit.

I'm not sure if my eyes are making them pop up or the computer or if I'm insane. I'm sure it's the eyes though as one of my students said.

I see knives stabbing me and my bodies red and black like what I see. This frustration.

That hospital trip. I went through what she did. That girl. We rode at least 4 buses to get there and when we did get there, I felt better. The beeps inside. The hell trip. God's angry and will send me there. I couldn't snap out of it.

Knew

Nude

New

Don't walk around _____!

I _____ you would walk around nude.

That's the point as well. To frighten people and know I am, even though they will act like they don't see anything.

They will act nonchalant. The point, to beat any pain they can cause. And to do it with nothing really.

To give them the same amount of pain they would've given me and more, but I want to do it better.

They wanted me to shoot myself, well I want them to do the same.

They deserve to off themselves.

For the pain they wanted me and my family to endure.

The _____ way to do things is not always the best way to do things.

I have to drill in that these robots are flawless.

It's a dangerous game we play. These lies. They're all dead. They are all dead.
Left for dead. Trying to snap her only girl out of suicide.

Captured.

Done.

Everything meaning yes and no.
Why would I care about anything?

It's Showtime.

No

Know

Note

I'm counting on my family.

I wouldn't care about anything if only being sold to robots.

Ghost. Done. This is final.

Done.

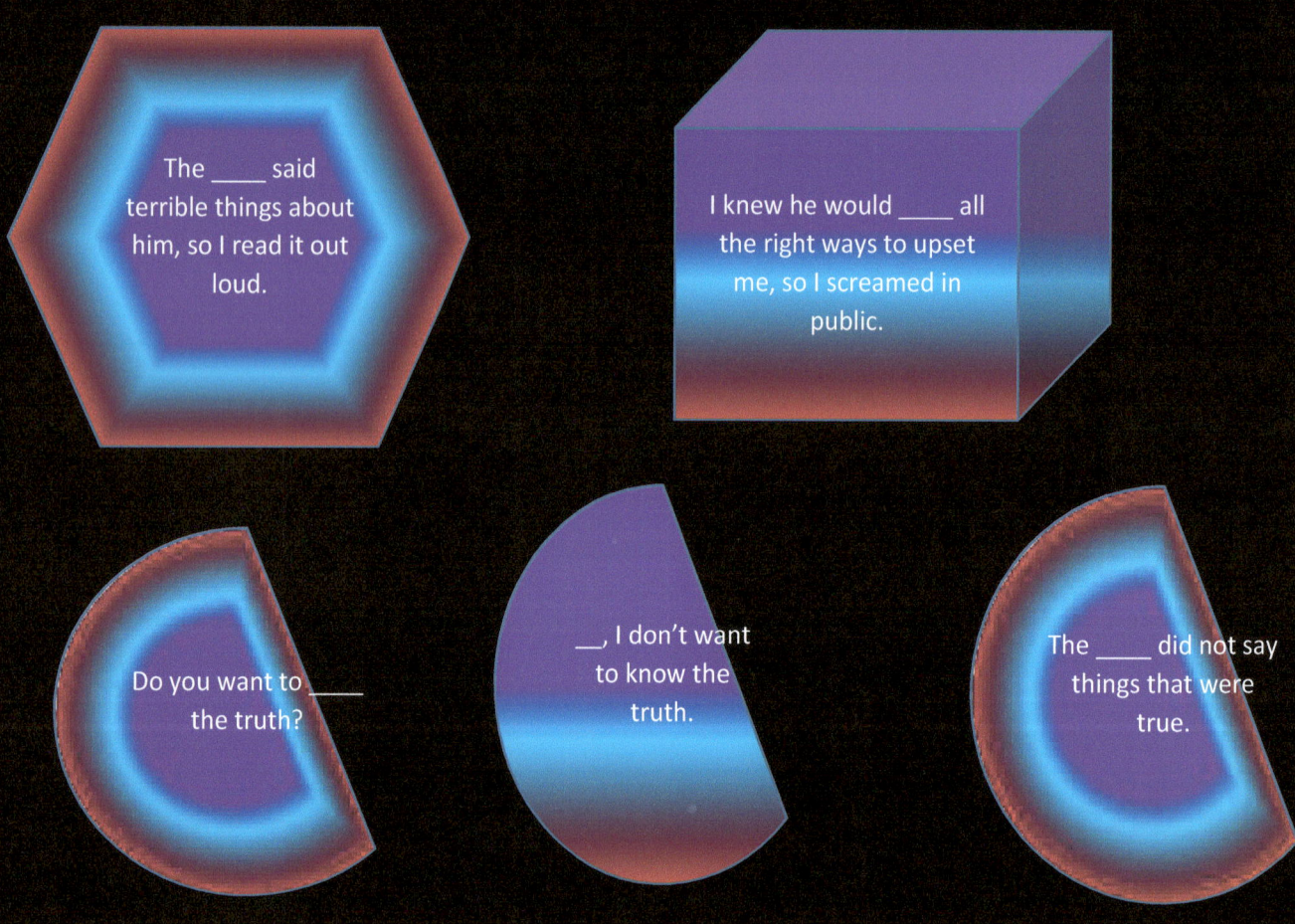

Fruit for dinner.

Legends!

The escape.

Families only child.

Trust and weight.

Creeps up on you.

To feel what they feel.

Need a new email.

I write with my _____ hand.

Adoption
These people that never thought they would experience suicide.
These people that never thought they'd experience slavery.

It came right in.

Who's watching me?
They're obedient to their masters.

Write

Right

Are you going to the left or _____?

You're doing everything the _____ way.

These people make every negative event you've experienced come to mind and play over and become continuous with the

Parents and older people that have experienced this chaos get furious. Popups of evil people in the brain just in every spot that's annoying, and fits their character; people with sense know too much of it can mess up your mental stability or cause death in sleep.

Parents that know those things happen get furious when their child speaks of events that can cause them to have breakdowns.

This shit is beyond me.

They know and can feel that help is on the way.

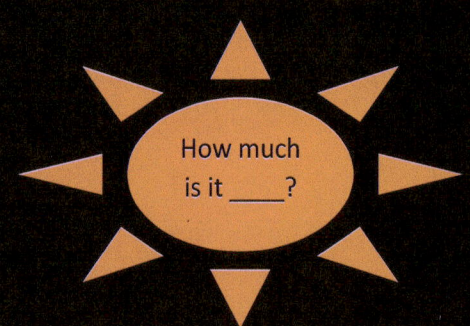

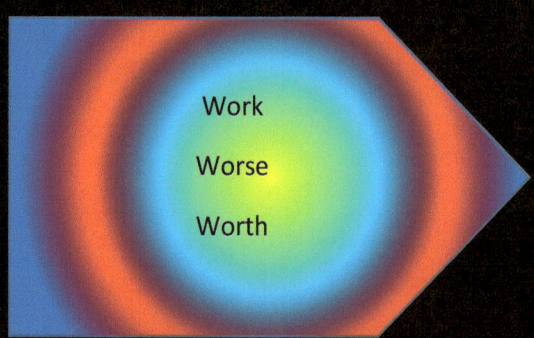

They're obedient. T hose evil people are in their faces right now.

Constant battle of suicide.

He couldn't pick his head up. That's how bad the pain was. Or the unsustainable conditions make the body.

Legends.

Constant battle of feeling alone.

Like going off on the deep end. But I have a balancer. A steady pacer/maker. An even mate.

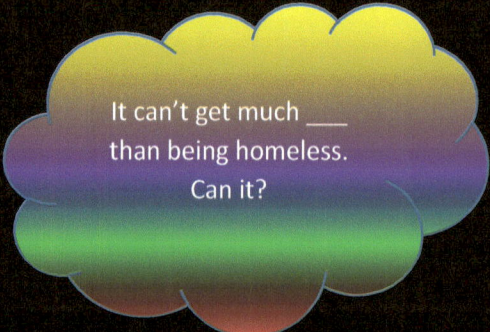

Mellower. Family stops me from getting to a point of jumping with reminders or any type of suicide.

Shaking bones, bumps, twitching like electricity shocking you. But natural.

It knows that I will get to that point. The game. The mellower. These robots that can feel me.

What's in you when you just click and commit suicide like it's a walk in the park?

These fucked up people gone feel it. Suicide. I know how it can be and still put in my robots to drive me as far as they could.

This pain goes on and on.

Sitting on hard things.

Trapped in cement box like things.

What doesn't kill my family will make us stronger.

Mom's strategy.

When

Win

Wind

_____ they wrote the documents in the beginning, of laws, was there any errors?

The _____ blew some of the pages away and they had to be rewritten.

How she kept 43, including Dad 44. Including her, 45 above ground.

No clue what my dad looks like or guess.

Need to watch videos.

This is all too much. Still.

Dad's strategy. I have no idea.

These people are bitter. Last feel of man and womankind. The beast want to see them. They work for it.

7/5-8/14 fast. Unless church food or offered from the library.

Let it burn.   We're doomed.

_____ will people learn that we've all been set up?

___ will things get back to the way God wants them?

Never!

Illnesses can develop from many things.
The first people need they asses beat.

Then all of this was for nothing.

Starting to feel my weight on Earth. It's an expression.

To feel regular. Not irritable or suicidal.

We have to save these people and evil and gruesome things have to be put in my mind.

Drilling in, experiencing suicide and aloneness on this level to get through or be able to see and help these people with no problem or constant up and down shit. Loneliness aloneness.

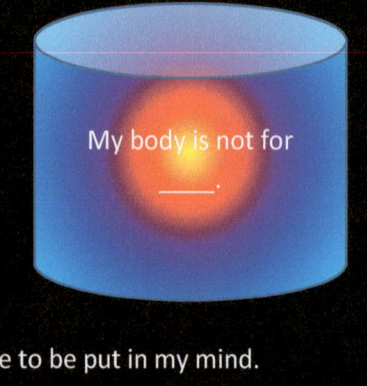

My body is not for
_____.

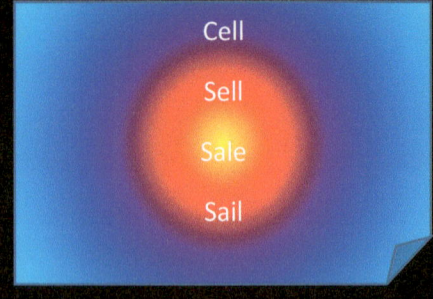

Cell

Sell

Sale

Sail

Still need that clamp.

To need to visit them so they can live or remind and give a feel to the ones that are going to pass away soon of what life was like above ground.

Standing cells. Porter potties. Being driven by.

Headaches.

Trying to get rid of a disease I see developing. Talking out loud.

Cries unknown. Keeps getting worse and worse. They're families are definitely not together. Real food falling. The want for it.

What would you do if you escaped from a _____ you were trapped in for over nine years for nothing?

Are the toothbrushes on _____?

I'm not going to _____ you anything because I don't like you.

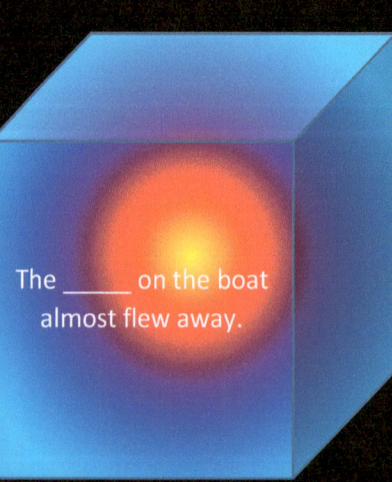

The _____ on the boat almost flew away.

The thought, hope, this shit, that one of your relatives got free and will come for you. It's good and bad that they are not together.

These bastards will pay for it all. I'm not leaving a decimal out.

Back to the lab.

Freedom out cages.

They need something.

We are all playing this game.

Using everything here to figure this shit out and for revenge.

4/15. Blood date. Why?

Including movie arrival, who sings what, robots writing something someone says and they see you and get mad. You write what someone says because it helps you remember something and they see you write it and blast you and get mad. Why they being nosy for one? Or are you? They are right next to you and you can hear them.

Boys learning girl's period dates and blasting them. Good night. That is trash. Discipline never given. Freedom of speech. You just get to irritate people. That's not Godly. Nor is it jail worthy.

It was useful to help you.

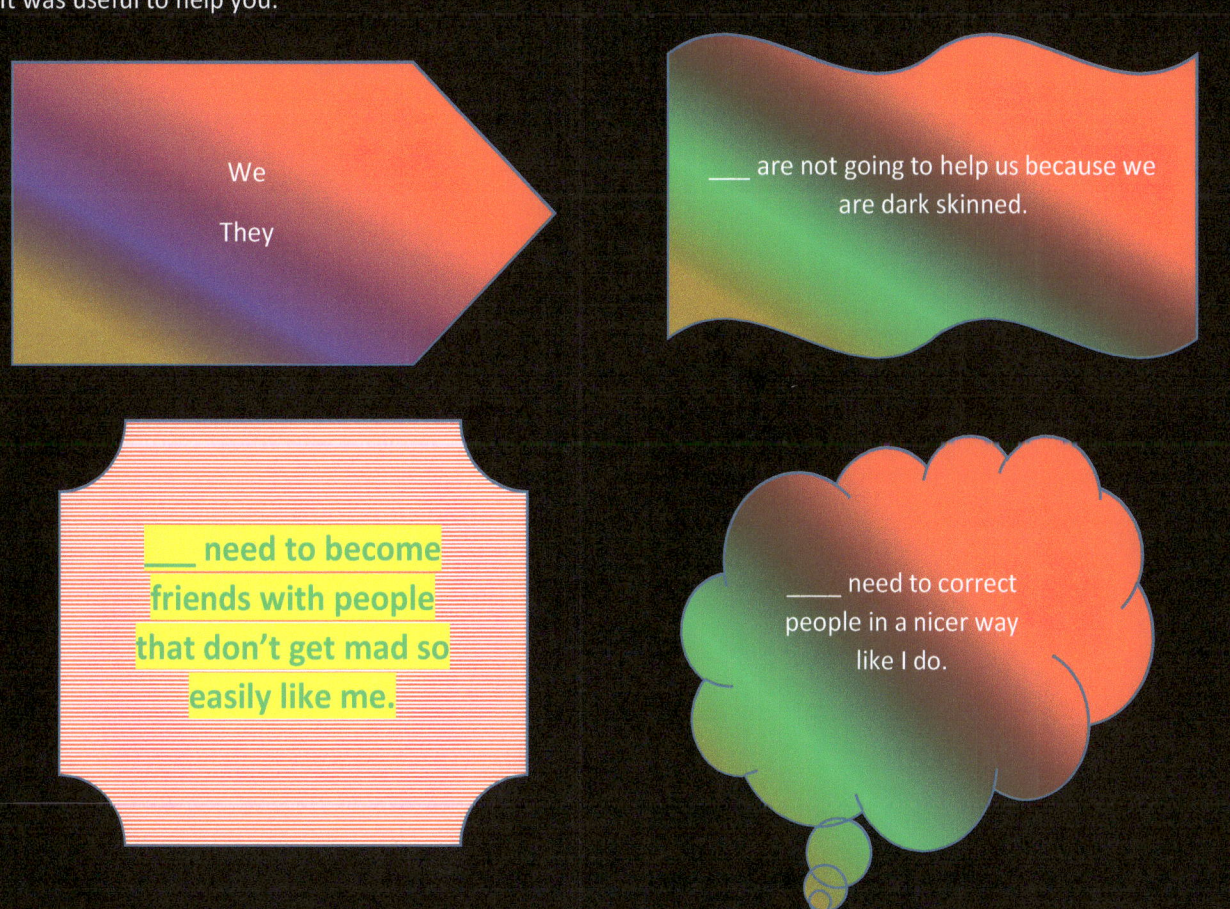

Sometimes Mom walks by.

They still envision their good life.

Coming back.

It's a live theater. They'll play out right in front of me.

What' they're going through will be live.

I have to put platforms there, like them coming up in shit and at tables, and other places to, well to act as cameras. And get the worst ways and conditions they could be in so when the real happens I won't even know, but I will, some shit like that, and my heart won't shake.

Preparation.

Still need to grasp that no matter what condition I'm in, the real is these people need to be freed and will have to start all over again. So their records.

Their criminal records are still there.

__ said don't disrespect his dick and I can live with that.

__ said it because he thought ____ would never let me enjoy it.

You know what ____ say, if you don't want to say it or admit it, just put it in a book.

____ both love to read about me.

How the hell do you get replaced and still have a record when you have a replacement that took your identity?

Doesn't make sense, but. Well put clues together that you've read.

Criminal record.

These people are out of their minds.

Some are dressed in animal skin.

He

They

We

Some women are dressed as men and in the cell of someone that is still breathing.

Some men are dressed as women.

They have to be the people that resemble them the most.

1. My _____ tells me that no one will believe most of the things I've written.
2. I'm in _____ pain daily experimenting with the revenge that my one year-old-self created.
3. Please _____ to read and I guarantee as the days go on, someone wil make a believer out of you.

Continue
Constant
Conscious

All of this to try and get closer to freedom.

There is a guide.

Like it or not.

There's 42 of them and I have to get used to seeing them one by one, because they were famous first.

Well they were my brothers first.

Some people have been eaten alive and the beast is still talking to them inside of it.

Some killed the beast and took its skin. The beast played dead (some were still inside of it) and relived. Some beasts just needed to wait for the organs to be replaced. Some were operated on.

I mean it. This is too much.

I have to remember:

Family is in this too.

They don't tell me what to watch or visualize.

1. You're _____, so please don't touch me.
2. What _____ were you born on?
3. My hair is in terrible _____ and it needs to be washed.

Contagious
Continent
Condition

That's me doing that.

Mommy wants to see how much her daughter will do for her. Or wants to do for her without her asking. She wants to know she's doing a good job.

I got projections surrounding me.

5:14PM 7/11/19. Thursday.

I said I was trying to reverse all the bullshit that was naturally put in me from the jump.

I said I was trying to fix body organs and shit that's fucked up and denying me everlasting life.

Going into deep comas. Pulling myself out of my skin. Believe. I've found a way to do it. When I was young. All types of illnesses we are all born with, I got rid of.

I said I was trying to get back everlasting life.

Why would God create us so we could die? He's too good for that.

Thanks pal. For the pat on the back.

I'm lying. But I said life should be eternal on Earth. And it can be. Just don't get hit by a car.

And go under all types of comas that yank you out of your sleep to be fixed.

Why get a shot for a disease you've never had? I'm not.

Ya'll have no idea how mad I am. I need this money.

These crazy people, well not so crazy.

They make these people act out all the annoying shit they've done in their dreams, thoughts, head over and over and make them do it in pain.

They make them act out the shit they do naturally.

1.   I don't want that bicycle that is in terrible _____.

2.   You need to put some _____er in your hair immediately!

3.   Don't try to _____ me to be your slave.

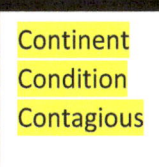

Continent
Condition
Contagious

They beat they ass until they bleed.

I mean. They just don't see a person.

These robots.

Some people are already computerized. They talk and walk. I mean. That means they are cameras, or can be at least, and a tape is playing over and over in their head of the headaches these people are.

Their memory is the damn chip that makes them or whatever the hell is in them to let them talk and see and move and change faces.

That shit is crazy.

How the hell am I just putting their eyes in the computer? They can see me.

The kid's dad stayed in the forest with him the whole time. I want to say that is me. All types of natural things are needed to get the body into eternal shape.

It's like I'm snapping them out of their consciousness.

Holograms.

I know my family has extra keys and buttons. This shit is getting on my nerves.

Okay. Whatever is not written, it's all in here. I said that. 1,2,3.

Just imagine what these people did to these so called humans that are capable of making your stomach turn and you to have miscarriages because they are so annoying. And stupid. And have issues with people that are darker colors.

It's unimaginable.

Just a headache.

They don't know, I don't know, how anyone can be so annoying.

Sit back and relax and enjoy all that is here to offer. 729.

Family organizing robots to snap me into knowing I have a family and who they are.

These robots are supposed to answer me. Give me answers to questions I have. I said that a while ago. But now I know I have to get used to that or my heart will keep having issues. Pumps, strains, stop for a second.

1. My _____ tells me to do good things, and these weird people that think bad is good come around and I want to hit them.
2. Which _____ is the most beautiful to you?
3. Is poison ivy _____?

Contagious
Conscious
Continent

Recorded sporadically. 43 – doubles. Done.

Was it worth it to learn what these robots can do? Where'd the money come from to take care of all of them? Permanent up and down rollercoaster.

Yes.

All these people do is make people argue.

The events (negative) make a puzzle and story in your mind naturally. The hell.

Twins. For each person and some of the things/events combine.

Think positive. Not how evil, racist want you too. Racist can be of any race.

The feeling of thinking everyone thinks you're dead and knowing there's been a good strategy for it to work and be believable.

Control

Conclude

Construction

You cannot _____ that fast ass girl you made.

I want to _____ this page by saying I wish that fast ass child of yours named Matenson was dead.

I'm doing _____ on my brain, and the only way to clear it of her annoying ass ways is to write negatively about her.

Platform adds to the story. – the more they're shown. Visitation – help is on the way.

Inventions never thought of. Hard to believe such things can be created. Done

Hard to believe there's these huge families and I'm in one of them.

Pure hell. Silent Whispers of instructions.

To feel what they feel when I'm there.

Synthetic. Hold on to me. God's 1 child.

Earthquake. Slaves freed and trapped some masters.

Discipline self with books.

I need to get back inside of my mind.

Here to figure out why?

4/15 blood date.

Why?

Control

Construction

Conclude

Those that want their kids to act like hoes need to have _____ done to their brains.

People that get angry. People aren't for things they'll never talk about doing. It's caught on tape. Trash.

11=ii

11=LL

11=ll – does this look like two (LL) or two ii's? Issues with the first documents.

Number letter connections. Tricks in the language. That ass will be beat and good.

This is the shit you want to do to my family and these trifling ass women to my brothers. And these stupid men to my brothers. It's going down. The whole place is in. Face mergence. This would be for nothing. I don't need this shit.

Some people with professional jobs using their practice to try and make you suicidal. All the knowledge they gained. Some people get jobs to try and locate the people that wronged them.

Tommy needs to _____ his paper by saying he's sorry.

Sometimes the only way to _____ my thoughts is to release the negative ones on paper.

To

And

Want

Make

Dose

Tooth

Some people want their kids ____ act fast as hell and sit around and play stupid, until the child feels violated of some sort.

Those kids need ____ be sent ____ the exact place they are trying _____ get the adult sent ___: prison.

Sometimes I let my brain keep getting frustrated until I figure out why it won't shift __ something better, and in this case, my thoughts kept getting worse so I would put real names in this book.

Myself is trying to keep myself alive.

Need a hug from my real family.

Now I feel like I have a fucking forest growing around me. Like paint. The point, to stay in reality. I will be seeing all types of shit. And I need to be able to look at these robots, myself, and answer them as if I see nothing.

This is war. And a reminder.

A good reminder. My head is answering my thoughts. All this shit. I need to get my act together.

Now I know the importance of stress balls and rubber bands on the wrist. I don't know who my family is.

Need to keep moving.

They're beat.

Looking at more robots.

I'm beat.

You can't call the police on situations like this. Shit like this makes people go overboard and their minds naturally get conditioned ____ do things ____ get rid of the problem.

Things with limbs that stretch out. 2 heads, eyes in the front and back.

These hard images.

The more of platform I do, the more I can feel them.

The fact is I'm tired of doing it, and have a hard time, my mind is just so damn brilliant.

Standing in awkward positions.

Would be writing all day.

Lots of evil per beast.

4/15. Blood date.

Per person.

Human animals. Hell no!

This is the shit they want to scare me with?

Want my brothers to see?

They need/want to be shot. Down there those people are so scared.

Hell rooms.

Platform telling more.

Now are they alive and is food given?

Escaping.

Family playing this game too.

They don't tell me what to watch. I watch it on my own based on how I feel. Everything helps.

5:21pm 7/11/19.

Clothes.

Innocent people being messed with.

Help is in there. My robots.

Family beating themselves up.

Stressing. To snap me out of feeling low and hopeless.

Things with bombs that stretch out. Huh? 2 heads, eyes in the front and back.

That ass whooping couldn't come fast enough. Places need to be found. Uh huh. Keep reading and FOLLOWING along.

I had _____ teach me these hard lessons.

____ this damn screaming in my head is getting on my nerves!

The hellish events keep _____ worse and worse. Longer and longer the real scenarios get with fake events that haven't even happened. These people, chaotic people, deserve to die.

The child started _____ frustrated in her private parts so she started being rude to the adult that was not giving her the pedophilic things she wanted, and the mom allowed the child to be rude, knowing exactly why the child was upset.

Robots
All
Getting

Things like this. Being put in rooms with nothing but kids because they act like kids, or it is known they've done inappropriate thing s with them. Forced to do them again.

Made to hate what you like.

Robots making me forget things.

They're separated. Things falling everywhere.

Still have to do them. Food clothes.

These are the last writings.

The good events that _____ in your life turn into bad ones. You're so frustrated that now it seems that all those good reactions were really bad ones.

They have to do evil to eat. Get a small taste of something humans eat. And at a maximum level. Beasts that want to look like them with terrible features. 3 titties. Shit like that.

Evil to eat.

These evil _____ made these people act out every good family event they had over, and in a bad way.

Different events telling me certain _____.

I said some of these people were beat and had no negative thoughts about the free because they know if we were all trapped, they'd be down there forever.

We'd all be down there forever.

I always wondered if I was down there, would I have the supplies to, well hell no. They gone pay for that too. I'm still trying to figure out how I did this shit and why.

Every second these peoples _____ change.

Parents
Thoughts
Things
Bastards
Happened

I said family was trying to pretend that they were beneath the ground trapped and they're not.

These mutha fuckas gone pay for shit that I make up. They so fucking done. I'm mad as hell at this shit.

Can't remember a single hug I gave my brothers.

5:21PM 7/11/19!

_____ were forced to say they regretted their children and even worse things. The most evil people alive captured them.

Why the hell would manevil go so far down to the bottom of the Earth that they couldn't breathe? Why would the beast want them down there? Does the beast want them all dead? Hell no. It gets a kick out of watching them suffer and needs them to make it feel good since it hates looking like a beast. Gassing up a beast, meaning making it feel beautiful.

Comma

Communicate

Commitment

"You need to use a _____ to separate things in your long sentence," a rude Mr. Chrisp said.

You need to _____ that you will help her a little better.

Basically I am trying to get sleep every night until this money comes.

I need my old job back. Time. This means I have to go to that office a few more times.

5:21PM.

I don't like this game.

Blood needs to be shed for this.

The real slaves down there surviving. The real! The ones that's taking that pain and still breathing. Never gave up on being granted freedom. Finding freedom.

I love my mommy!

Mr. Sharp made a _____ to help her.

I said these people would want me, everyone to experience they're hell that they deserve. All these gnats.

They really ain't shit.

Literally every time you think of them a bad scenario pops up.

And now they're dealing with the crazy people they prescribed.

Dialogue, and with their sorry ass kids, keeps getting longer. You expect, your brain naturally gives them the worst scenes. Fucking gnats.

And its' real.

Common

Command

Commit

Commend

I _____ the mother for never letting her child stay trapped in a mindset of being alone.

Having fourty-three kids is not _____.

Staying in reality. Shaking the world. Done. Chaos.

No projections. Clearance. Diseases every day. Drugs. Drink. Be normal.

Visitation – help is on the way.

Looking in mirrors and calling themselves ugly. Done. Yes this plays a part in your stability, forced to do it or not, and takes a toll on your brain.

Done. Bad side conversations about spouses caught on tape. Done. No. Not caught. On purpose. Mean folks.

Is it _____ that people you despise keep popping in your brain?

I have to _____ to finding out what the fuck happened to this place.

I _____ that everyone evil that is living be trapped in a lifetime of pain.

They're still down there doing all those devious things I've envisioned.

Feels like I'm seeing things.

Chaos.

We're watching you. We're coming for you.

Sometimes things will be left out and considering these flawless robots, they were meant to be left out.

I love my brothers!

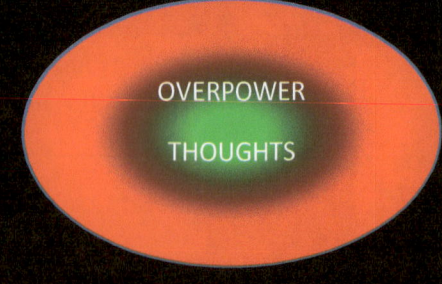

OVERPOWER

THOUGHTS

I need a clamp that makes it mandatory to visit these people every day. I don't have it. Just an, are they alive? If I get the emergency call needed, even though they still trying to lure me and my brothers, Mom and Dad down there, I will do what I need to so they can get out as soon as possible.

I know the pain must be killing them.

Hell no. These people exist. And this type of pain medicine is given.

Hell no.

> Now I'm to a point where I'm recognizing that I want to act out these fucked up events in my _____ instead of overpower them with positive _____ and get them out of my mind.

I mean it. These people are a complete headache. But I think.

No I have to drill in that they have paid in full for everything they've done.

1. Robots.
2. Projections.
3. Movement/further in escape.
4. Dispensing food, clothes, needs.
5. Platform to feel like in the facility.

> I need to come up with a chant, or something to recite as quickly as possible to_____ these events.

I'm supposed to visit them every day like a job.

I'm projecting them and have to remember it's not a mental illness seeing people.

This is to save them. I'm doing this on purpose and can't talk about it.

These low lives. And now they know. What people want to do to low lives.

To them, with looks, to them.

Evil people have no looks to me. They just need to go. But these particular ones have paid in full for what they've done.

So if the monsters minds are computers, they talk and shit, does this mean they are constantly recording and remember and storing all the information they see?

Bring it with the hell is what they said to these bitches. They put them through worse trauma.

You want to give people headaches, we'll give you one. And they basically let them know the only way they deserve to live, is to not be considered human. And in that case, all others don't deserve to live. Something like that.

They're made of shit and they know it. And they're bitter about it. Really!?

Momma be on point. Still trying to clamp in this shit. I couldn't sleep that well last night. But I made it after struggling a little. I need some income. 8 hours a day it will have to be. 11:51PM.

And they deserved it.

They don't know where the hell these things came from, or how or who created them. They work just like humans. Well look like us at least.

They refuse to let them take their lives. They refuse to let them take over the world.

Integrity. And pride.

Pride and Integrity.

The things I'd do to figure out all the hell someone wanted to cause me. And I need to _____ to add names in this book. That's part of the reason I keep frustrating myself too. I'm under a spell I prescribed myself.

Watching TV like it's a webcam. In 3D. The best of the best.

It's like they're live. And they really are. All eyes in. Holograms.

I mean really. I have to fucking watch the damn people that did evil to them because they get on my nerves too. I need a cooler. Cool down method.

Yes, I want to know all the _____ these fucked up people wanted to prescribe me.

Half-crazy. Going crazy.

It's just best to say I'm related to no one and my family left me and everyone's dead .

Wait let me explain.

So no episodes.

To no one and my family left me and everyone's dead.

DISEASES

REMEMBER

Family can't rush being seen. Heads will build up. I'll explode. Mind collapse.

I said these people were killing people in their sleep. Not literally, unless deserved, but the negative shit they did or do to them still builds up in their daydreams and sleep and they collapse.

Seldom. Told to say they don't want kids. A lot!

Mom works hard to snap me out of suicide.

It's all in here. 1,2,3.

Animal land.

Kingdom can.

POSITIONS
SOMEONE
PHRASE
EVERY
SCREAMING

They wanted them to forget _____ good memory.

They had to hold the exact sex _____ in pain.

747.

In the middle of the night I need to do projections and watch footage.

I need a place to stay for all that though.

That diet resolution after the fireworks, I didn't do it.

I felt fat as fuck earlier. Like obese and I know I'm not, even if I want to be smaller.

And a professional might tell me I am in the range of the right weight.

I hate when ugly people who know they are ugly say cute things to me. It's no longer a pretty word or cute _____.

Maybe they think they're cute. _____ lied to them. All I say is so.

I love my brothers.

Some heard cries and didn't go all the way.

I said they sit around and wait for/on me.

1,2,3. Believe it.

Career for me.

I'm _____, and at myself: a hologram. The things I'd do to someone causing me this type of pain.

Robots act like the real people.

Trapped and in pain (some sort of pain) 24 hours.

My mom keeps saying, with her looks, don't disrespect her when I say I'm not hers during my phases.

This up and down rollercoaster.

All pure hell down there.

Slavery.

Slavery and to animals.

Do the masters have a section?

Black beasts, animals feel terrible and let the world play out how it was. Whites on blacks, blacks surrendered then they need to act like they have pain.

I made it up.

Fiction.

Made 1. Rush El. He.

Told there's only 1 and there's more than 20 of some man and woman's kids.

Might turn out to be.

Keep holding on.

All the days I've been _____ and I'm hanging and forced to believe I will make it and there's a strategy.

I'm forced to believe the money is coming. It's not for nothing. This up and down _____ that is.

Every day they have to act beyond evil because they are scared they will die. Natural human _____.

The point in the process is to understand what the slaves are going through.

NEED

ROLLERCOASTER

SUICIDAL

TENDENCIES

I do not _____ to do the platform as often.

I love my Mommy!

Trapped in pain (some sort of pain) 24 hours. Balloons. Demands of slaves met little by little with tourists, but smart to know.

10-23-22/10-24-22.

Relax. With these up and down rollercoasters. Monsters. Slave owners. Breathing – a little above rock bottom. Hills, up and down. Air. Battling suicide is not what I signed up for. Racist. The scheme to get everyone to rock bottom.

Circle of people.

How can she stand by me and I keep having phases and people are trapped?

Okay, so the constant annoyance of events _____ longer and things getting worse and worse all because you are an annoyance and hate me, are really enough.

I mean I can _____ why people would set your face on fire. They don't see a human. Someone who feels pain.

So I'm running to those visuals I see of myself and talking through them as well as _____ into the situation that visual is in. So I'm really having two conversations. These diseases.

These people that have lots of races/ethnicities mixed in them and their kids come out different colors.

Some are rude and assume that the mother was a hoe. Others have sense. These small common sense things naturally knocked out of us because people want to hold in shit they should talk about, like why someone grew 2 inches overnight and is sitting in the same seat in the classroom as the person that was 2 inches shorter yesterday.

The day prior.

And they have a variety of colors on their kids.

These people have fake skin on their faces. It's going down. Upon _____ date.

I love my Mommy!

I love my Daddy!

Getting

Understand

Release

Today

I love my Mommy!

I love my Daddy!

Legends!

My conscience. Okay _____ I realized that I am 7 years olds. Or I could be 7 going on 8 on December 25th.

I need to clamp everything in and start celebrating on the _____ dates. Are my brother's birthdays really those days?

I did say that some_____ had false information on them as far as birthdays. It's easy to type something wrong on purpose on a birth certificate.

1. Have to travel to different parts of. Stay here. Thoughts. Platform.
2. Watch different videos.
3. Platform if I feel like it. (family trying to get me to realize I'm bigger and have created things bigger than what I know) (far beyond average intelligence)
4. Puzzles. They will tell me what to watch and help me clamp in the truth.

Naturally Designed. My platform. To give everyone a second chance. The place. The platform. Humans. Humanity.

I feel like that baby is in me now. 42.

I have a lot of _____. Time to play games. I know their birthdays are right in front of me. I've done too much with numbers. 125 is the talent number.

Correct

Documents

Brothers

Images

Worrying

This shit is real. The only way to get rid of those ridiculous_____ of those hideous creations is to see things that naturally distort them and make them vanish in your mind.

_____ of shit that hasn't even happened with people you don't know.

Bottom line, they have paid well past capacity for their actions.

People that died because of things they said or stole or did to them, their hearts were weak to begin with.

The story keeps extending. The fight. To go. Ir.

Jealousy of big families. From people too lazy to have that many. 9 months is a lot per child. Some people can't have any

They had to tell these people they hate, that they love them. I mean it. They are angry._____ footage? I never thought about this part being recorded. Uh oh.

Recorded

Fucked

People walking around thinking they're better than others because they are lighter is _____ up. Do you care that their skin was burned?

Push it out. Get rid of it. All that damn arguing.

People ruining the entire day for others.

Speak on it then.

All that damn arguing amongst each other.

These people have no idea how this equipment works.

So they have no idea if I'm working as fast as I can.

They have no idea if I'm taking advantage of them. They should know how or what taking advantage of people is. They do it well. This fuckery. Only applying it to their needs and not their annoyances to other people. And not changing it no way.

Family knows though.

I can feel the blood moving in my scalp. This shit is awful.

Got damnit!

Get back to not giving a damn what these people think.

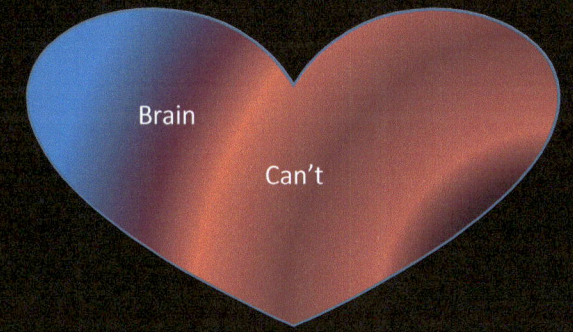

If I am 6, it's really going down. I just _____ figure out how this makes things worse for me and my family though.

How the hell can someone create something or do something to themselves to shoot that they are 30 years old in their _____ when they are really 6?

These are the same people. I have them walking around and acting the same way as the real ones when they were alive. Or maybe they still are. No wonder I feel so much suicide.

Or is it because I'm bad off right now, that I pay attention to all the negative things?

The trance is real. I'll go overboard. The need to get revenge on these savages. For what they would do to me and my family

Legends.

Here.

If I really am 6, _____ those people that have been down there for over 13 years, and are just getting help, are strung out of their fucking mind.

What you see on TV will be different than what someone else sees.

This type of shit. You just get to cause hell and enjoy all the new things that life has to offer.

It's flawless.

We're chipped.

You're chipped.

That person, that person you need to see to make your face cringe.

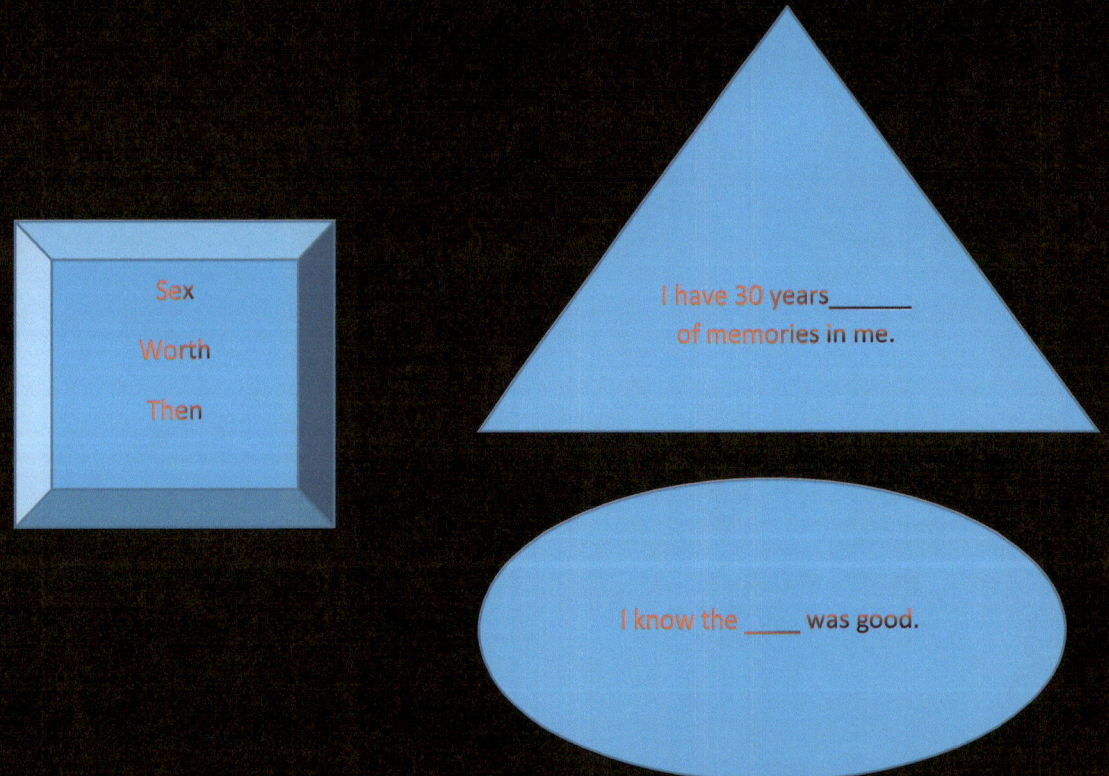

Sex

Worth

Then

I have 30 years_____ of memories in me.

I know the _____ was good.

I mean it. These mutha fuckas done found a way to make the whole population, except for a few vanish as if they never existed. It's like you get sucked down there and there's shit going on up here to make it seem like you never left. Like you're a damn ghost. All these lies right here. The ones full of gossip that was thrown around. All the hoes you slept with. "Oh he's over there."

Training yourself to want to be bad and messy? Look at one of the ways you caused yourself to never be gone. People lying and saying you're there with them, (granted by now you know I'm smart enough to know that some people you have done nothing to and yet they will lie just to make you mad. Maybe they like you. Maybe they're mentally ill.) I'm aware of this.) But you are responsible for a few things. Some of you.

When you cause _____ in people's lives by asking to borrow money and never paying it back, you do deserve to be punished. And since it is unlikely you will be arrested, the people you wronged just may hold you hostage.

He had to _____ really hard while cutting his penis.

Concentrate

Concentration

Conflicts

My _____ is blown that these so called good looking folks that ruin lives and think it's cute to gossip, really got taken.

They really thought no one would come up with something to make them suffer.

Creations that they can't put their mind on how it got created. The first time they heard an animal talk. Heart attacks.

These people have had to sleep in doghouses.

Real shit. These families. These people that think they're just so perfect and have the best looking kids and are just rude to people. They think it's cute to gossip and get on people's _____ at times. Some of this shit they think turns their man or woman on. Some of this shit they think is what naturally happens in all relationships and want their partner to feel that he or she is in a natural relationship.

This shit is beyond me.

Captured.
They are.

she

The blood numbers.

Your skin will feel weird. It can get out of control.

Technical. Technology like never before.

You'll hear whispers.

I lost a lot of weight and days went by, and I did all the work.
How can this be? 30 but really 7.

nerves

it

These people. It really happened. They were good to who they wanted to be good to and got captured by enemies. The only way to escape was to use the people that they didn't want to be around. Yes indeed. Torture. The Payback. The ones that fell for the stupid cry of help. I don't think anyone did. I think it made them more upset that these fools did them wrong and wanted their _____. Those fools figured that at least they would be with people that hated them that wouldn't kill them, if they transferred. They were wrong.

That famous store helps me out.
And there's many codes around that tell me otherwise.
Am I tall or not? The food does have many issues with it.

Messy and angry people working at these places.
Take the wheel. Drive.

Could be coming from anywhere.

Like your device in your ears while nothing is playing.

Implanted things all over.

This is a new day.

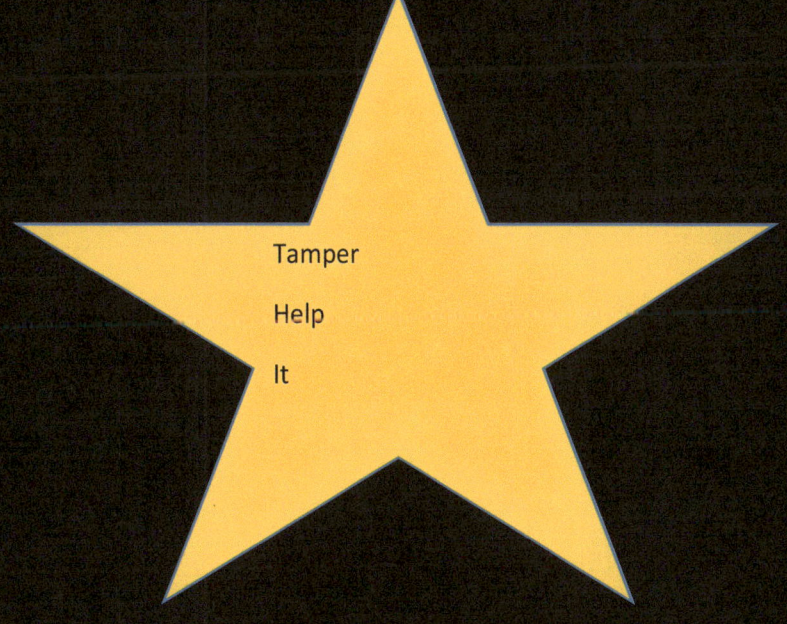

Tamper

Help

It

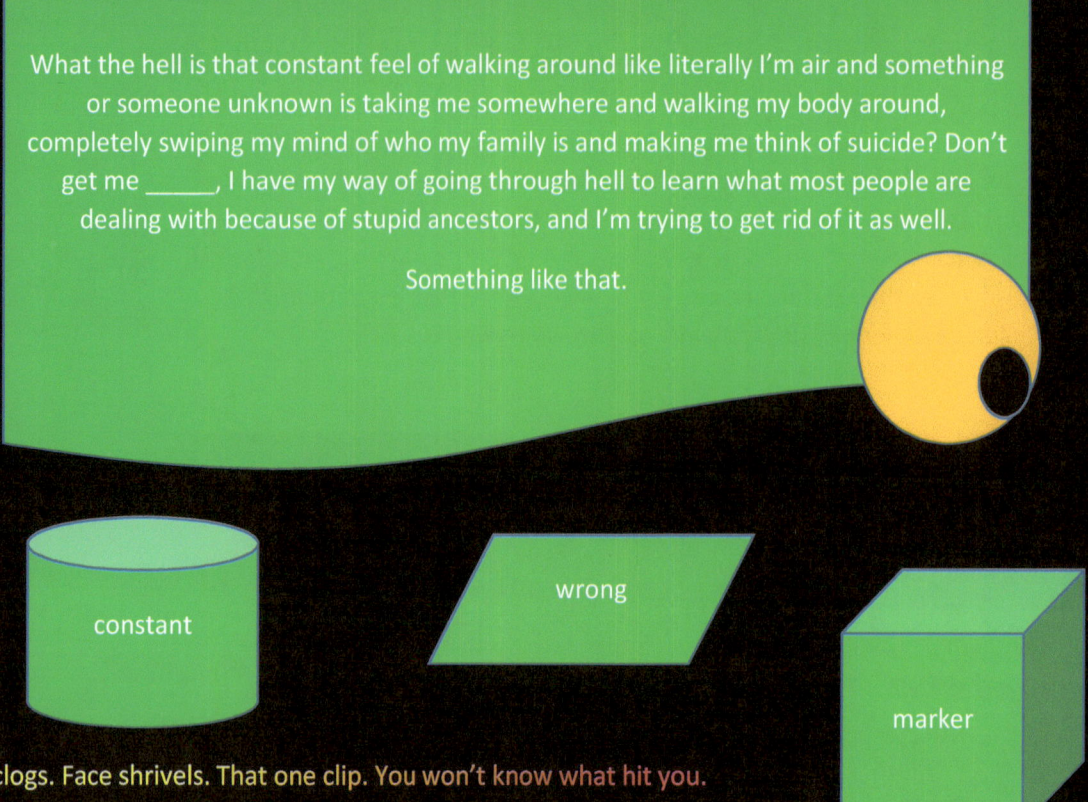

What the hell is that constant feel of walking around like literally I'm air and something or someone unknown is taking me somewhere and walking my body around, completely swiping my mind of who my family is and making me think of suicide? Don't get me _____, I have my way of going through hell to learn what most people are dealing with because of stupid ancestors, and I'm trying to get rid of it as well.

Something like that.

constant

wrong

marker

Blood clogs. Face shrivels. That one clip. You won't know what hit you.

145.

What you see on TV won't always be different. Different enough to bother you. Or just bother you because you won't say anything.

Robot ex-boyfriends, trying to get me to commit suicide in slick ways.

All this shit, I'm just figuring it out.

Is it that serious for her or him to leave you? Yes these new creations are crazy.

145.

This is war!

Legends!

Hidden snitches. Animal snitches. Rats. Said they were beating their kids up to perform well so I would come back.

Rats and birds that can hide in small spaces and blend in. Animals with different colors.

So I'd come back and watch another video.

This shit is unbelievable.

They have confirmations. Bitter. 10+years beneath.

I get tired of watching these damn clips.

These people are_____ in fucking cages. They can't even stand up in them.

sleeping

pump

mess

The thing about my conscious is, in these robots at least, it knows what's best. If these people have paid in full for their behavior, then it's squashed. The robots aren't fucking with their minds. In my opinion, with all this hell in my mind, they deserved it. No one did anything to them. If they shitted on themselves, that's they problem.

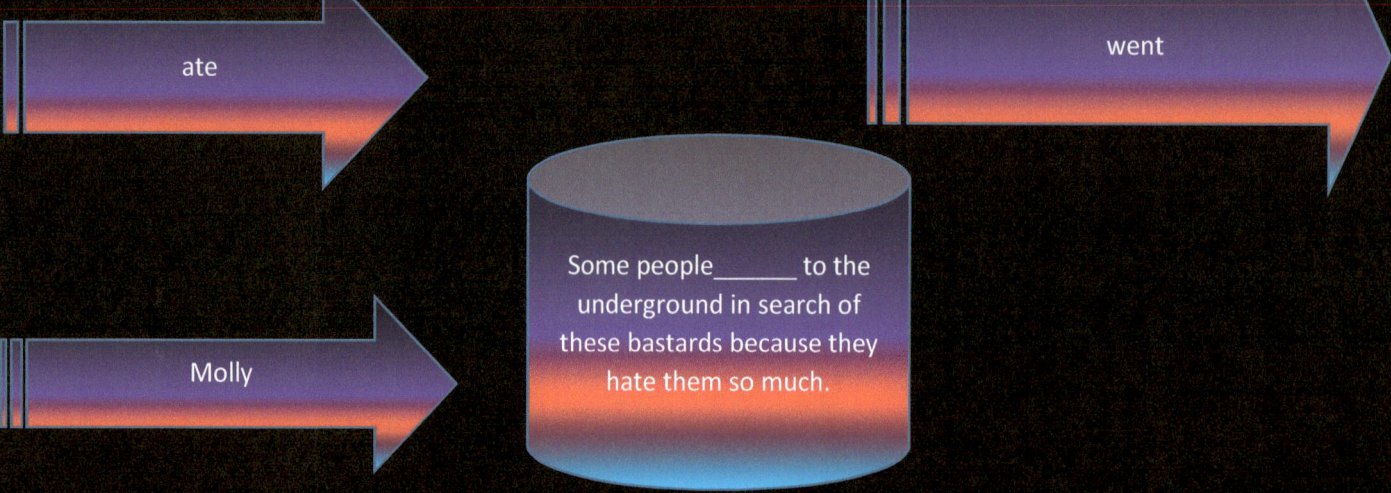

These people are going to come above ground and attempt to fuck up everything for everyone. They think some people are free and left them. Or not helping to get them out.

358, 108, 207, 754, 757, 210, 111, 624, 209.

The animalistic people or simply computer people are changing faces down there, scaring the hell out of them.

The point: a feel of human life.

I mean, I'm to a point where no punishment is good enough for these people.

I'm supposed to accept this game of tug of war.

It does voices of people they don't like and says things they say or have said to the people it bothers.

I mean it. I'm starting to think they are dead again.

Why do I feel him every time I hear that song? 2019.

2019.

Get back to not giving a damn what these people would think.

Just walk in that building full of thousands and know that all types of fucked up people are out there. Go out there and excel still.

The realist won't give a damn about a bad look.

Are they still with the human enemies?

Red?

Black.

Brown.

Yellow?

They want to get out now. Common Sense. Beige.

These people have me thinking someone is always looking over my shoulder.

Did this help me figure out what I want to do in life?

I mean it. All the studies in the world.

I'm no expert.

I can't believe you can get to a point of insanity where everyone just hops in spaces in your thoughts and does wrong. Especially real people that do you wrong and make it that much worse, and people that have never done you wrong. I mean is that everyone.

I'm not laughing, but I am.

It's hard to not

_____

on how fucked up certain people can be.

Conflicts
Concentration
Concentrate

I keep saying they have paid in full for all the _____ they've caused in people's lives.

My _____ is set on revenge. There's no way I have robots down there and these fucked up ass people aren't paying in some way for all the hell I have to find out.

Music bringing up projections.

Station to station they go.

The reasoning, meaning keeps getting deeper and deeper.

I said it hurt them to be in there with their siblings. TRAPPED!

ACTING in embarrassed ways.

I have to stay strong for that beautiful life I see.

Beautiful and handsome people catering to me.

Beautiful scenery.

Beautiful music.

They wanted to play stupid to so much shit and make people's lives so _____ that we can't even see them as human.

These robots already knowing what I'm going to do is on my nerves.

They turn into animals. More confirmation that bad comes soon. They are alive. Why would I need to make robots that can morph into anything? Wolves, foxes.

I did all this and ya'll just get to come up here and fuck it up because what?

Ya'll still ain't shit?

No one can _____ it.

They've _____ some people into nut cases. People want them dead. Through all the hell and injections they've been given, they lived.

Believe

Turned

Miserable

It hurts bad wanting to be a --man and you were born a -an. The things they would do. They know. They know their height is above what a -------man's usually is. They know those looks are ugly. Eating with their mouths opened and shit to irk you on purpose. The ways to put a chain of bad thoughts in your brain.

It will take time. I just can't see all. I will explode.

That shit there. Keep seeing 08 to grasp in myself and not get too upset that it's 09 and ++ of us plus me. You'll never understand this.

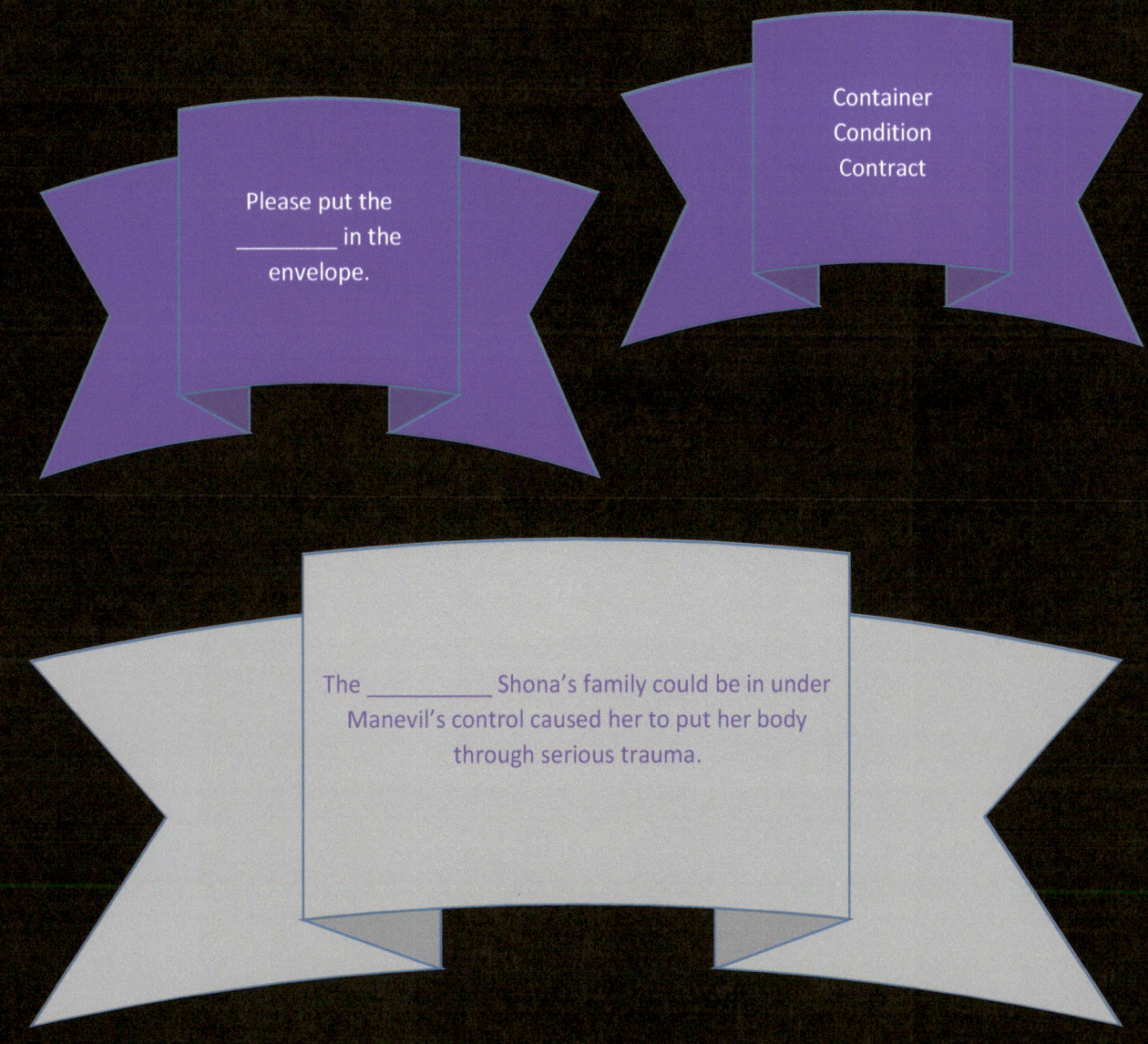

Please put the
_____ in the
envelope.

Container
Condition
Contract

The _____ Shona's family could be in under
Manevil's control caused her to put her body
through serious trauma.

Wanted help from people in high places. How long before the people in office realize we're gone? These people. They exist.

always give up and lose it all: family and they're alive, then Mom and brothers and Dad, who seems to be a ghost right now, realign the robots.

Worrying about a job. No money. More ways people forget you exist.

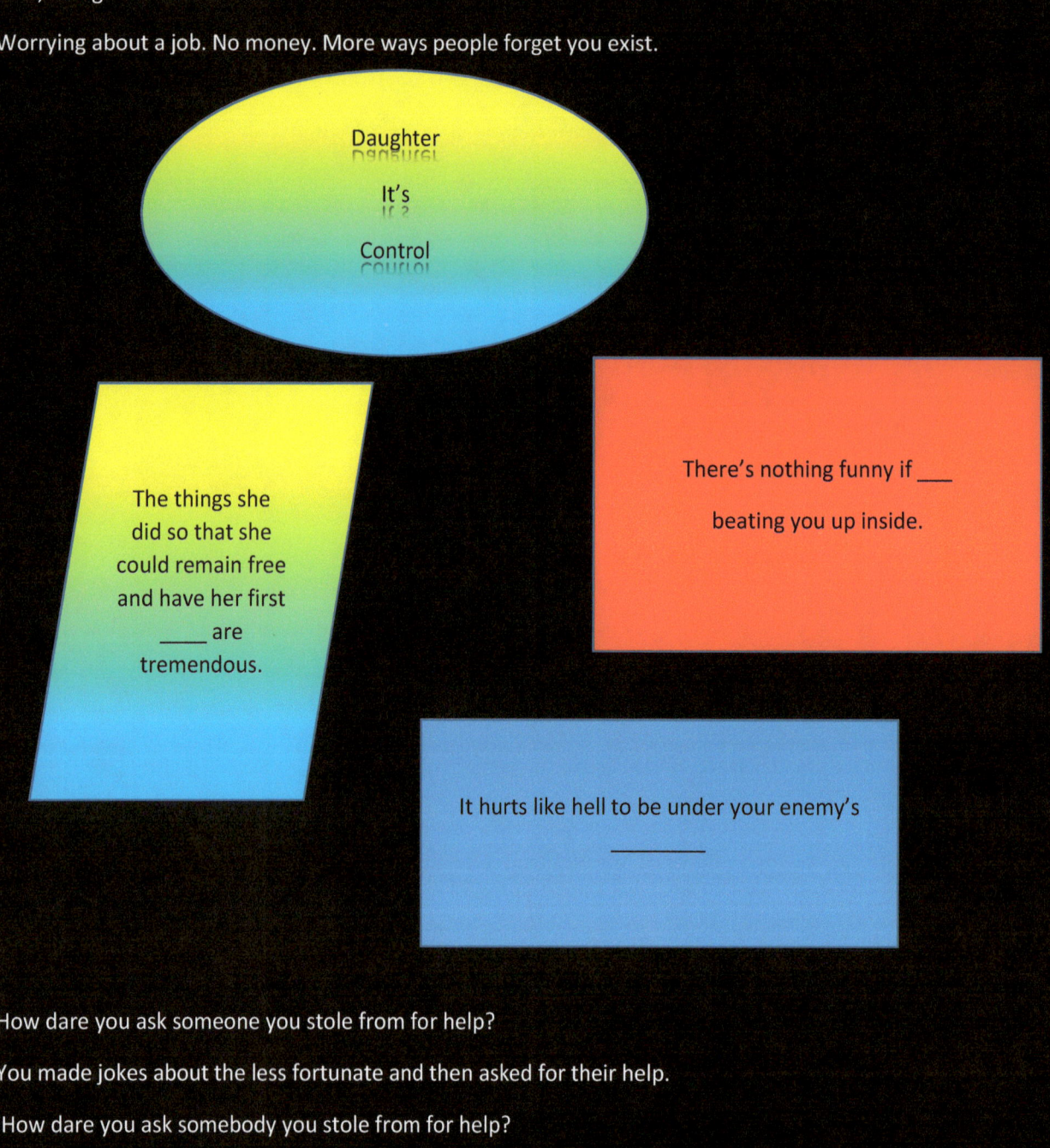

Daughter

It's

Control

The things she did so that she could remain free and have her first _____ are tremendous.

There's nothing funny if ____ beating you up inside.

It hurts like hell to be under your enemy's _____

How dare you ask someone you stole from for help?

You made jokes about the less fortunate and then asked for their help.

How dare you ask somebody you stole from for help?

Better situations. Less pain. Won't die. These lies. 7/13/19.

Circles of hell. Some kind of way this circle of bullshit is how they're alive.

These lies.

They killed him. He saw what they did. Now he's playing all types of crazy and it's working.

It's a man that looks like a woman. They started realizing certain things.

I have to keep_____ myself that the hell I put myself through is to know what it feels like (what the enemy is doing to people and wanted to do to me and my family) and to understand what's going to_____ to these evil people. It keeps getting worse because what innocent people went through and are still going through is so outrageous. Some people talked a good game. But I'm the only one that could back up what I say.

Happen
Reminding

Too many fucked up people. Getting on your nerves. These people around. With these people around. Death begins to sound good.

I'm no expert or doctor

I said I told these people some of them had each other's kids. Since birth

Mixed up families.

Babies mixed at birth. Purposely.

You see them two different areas, you know that person you said looked like another person. Exactly. They're probably related.

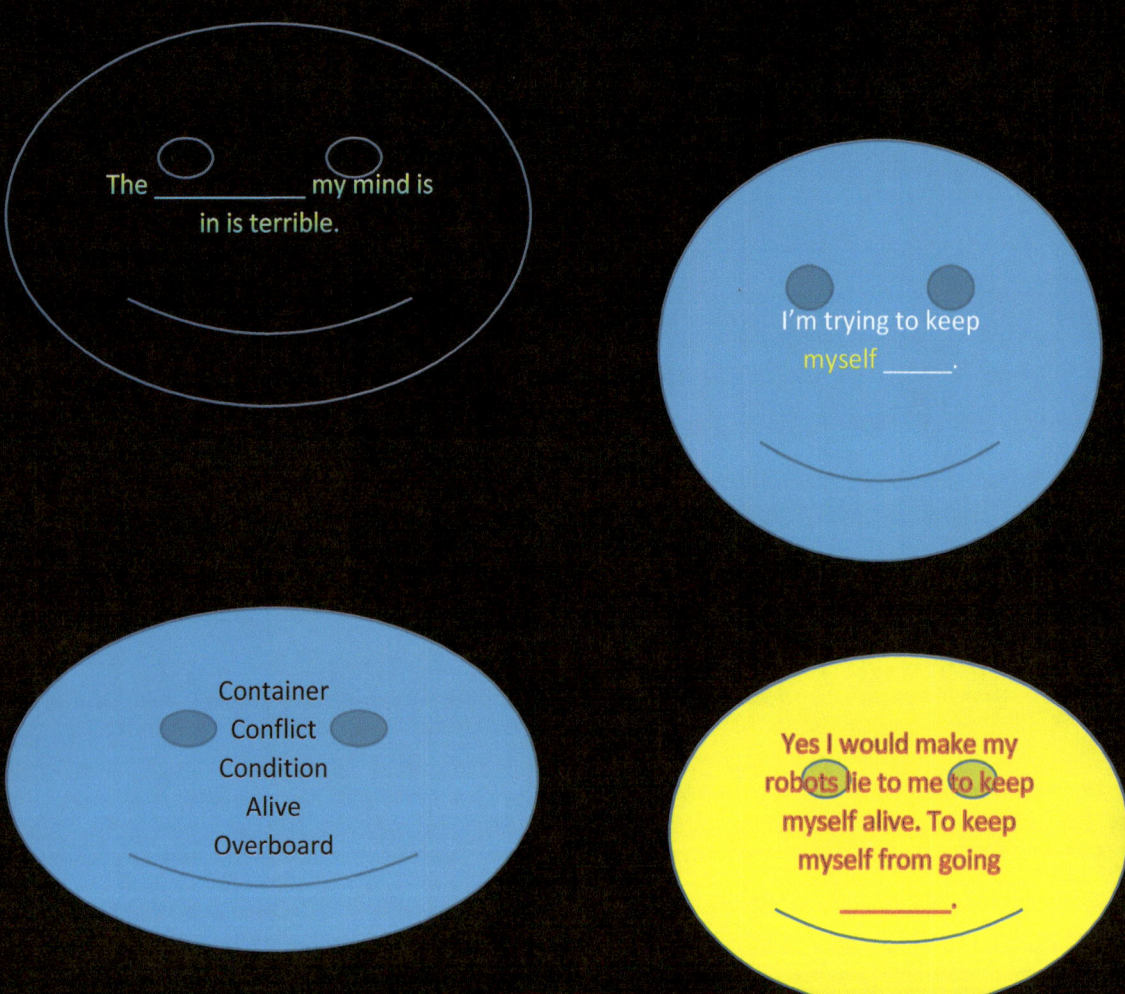

Identical.

Not being able to focus on work because of a headache.

These people are.

It's not funny anymore huh?

It's like I need to read a story to get my mind off their chaos.

There's an amount of videos, particular ones, that need to be watched or I'll be irked until I get the answer I need or sight through robots.

I said they were still down there lying to me. They want out. And were good to no one but who they thought qualified to them. Payback. It hurts huh? Will they do it again? Hell yea.

Now they know how hated they are.

The robot said read when I wrote it. Read.

It hurts like hell to know the entire, well almost all of the human population has been _____.

These people have had to shoot each and every part of their _____.

These people have had to shoot their _____on every part of their bodies.

Bodies

Defeated

Relatives

Their eyes are recording.

We're almost confirmed. My family # and they're alive.

Less suicide fell every day.

It's hard to grasp if these people are even still _____.

What the hell is that? One breath she's my mother and the next breath she's _____.

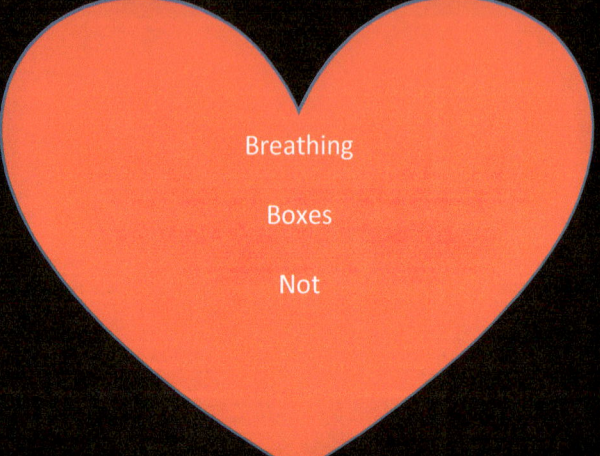

Breathing

Boxes

Not

These people have been put in _____like they were packages. They've even been put in suitcases.

Robots and family keep me afloat to know if they're alive.

How the game works?

Walking in and out of reality bubbles.

The lies to be placed with better. Less hellish situations.

The lies to be placed with less pain. Some would kill them.

The doctors they found.

The game. The game requires me to watch specific clips.

All animals in cages.

They put the humans in cages. People in jail. People in prison. Yea right.

The whole world has been living in cages since the... Well since.

For the last 6 years plus, the whole world has been living in cages.

Cells. Thin.

The length. Hmm. 9x6 is my book length. Maybe in feet.

8 by 11. May be too good.

Projections. Holograms.

Projections work.

All the ways I'm pulling myself to grasp in this body if they're breathing.

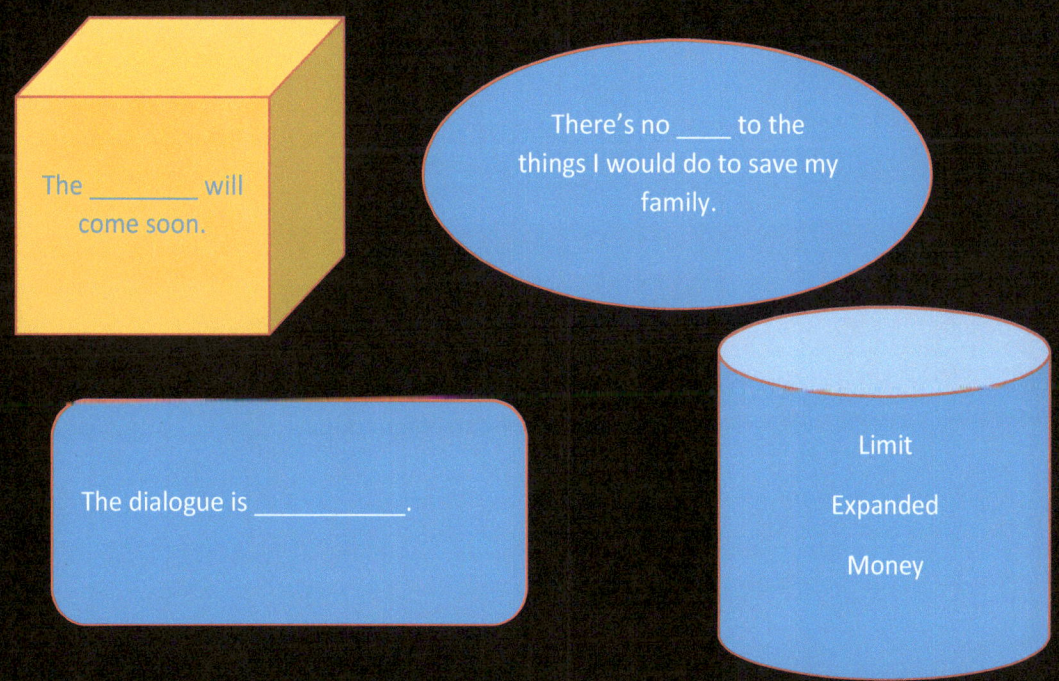

The _____ will come soon.

There's no ____ to the things I would do to save my family.

The dialogue is _____.

Limit

Expanded

Money

If you had to choose, maybe these would be the ones you chose to get rid of. Or take the most pain.

This book isn't done until the game rules are figured out. 10:19AM!

Is 2 cents an hour really that far off from 12 _____ an hour if it's been over 200 years?

I don't remember when _____ was.

If you ask me, we naturally were ____ into slavery. Never a chance to fully be able to do things we want to do without a guaranteed money burden.

Born

Dollars

Slavery

They hear them responding to them different.

They believe they feel genuine hate. There's no mercy.
The stories help me understand what happened to this place.
These people are completely manufactured. Noses, eyes shot? Believe it. The most hated. A trend against black women.

The only way to get out is to know where the hell they've been.

They have to do everything over and better. The beasts are conditioned.

Project Rescue.
Save Humanity.
Everyone.

Next scene and new title.

Surrendered to beasts. I mean it. I keep thinking I'm related to these damn popular people. And 42 of them at that. That number must just be for me to keep thinking of them and help the escape.

They're not at rock bottom.

Call the tax office for balance.

Find us!
Me, Abigail Joyce, and My Brothers!

1. Malcolm – blue on couch
2. Evan – black "only you know"
3. Leviticus – white "only you know"
4. Exodus – red and black jacket (Drink) "only you know"
5. David - that clap "I need you"
6. Cameron – the seat "I need you"
7. Maurice – blue (we're in this together)
8. Julliard – You won't keep disrespecting him
9. James – the bed (You know what you did – brother voice)
10. Johnathon - blue by the bars
11. Anthony – the alley – Yes Really
12. Jamal – coming out the spinning entrance/exit
13. Colton – nice eyes the seat (You know what you did)
14. Aaron – black and white looking like the picture (piano)
15. Justin – the interview (army in)
16. Jordan – green - Yo
17. Turner – Say hello, not goodbye
18. Carter – he's fire in that all white (It's really 5:50PM 8/15/19
19. Brandon – red (laughing) candy does taste good.
20. Miles – black (laughing) candy does taste good
21. Alvin – Loyal, black and cap
22. Porter – all black, that interview. Solid as a rock
23. Demetrius – do you mind, the piano
24. Clarence – the water, do you mind
25. Timothy – No lie no lie. Nice eyes
26. John – got damn boy. Hi brother
27. Jeremiah – practice interview
28. Sampson – black uniform
29. Raphael – I need a girl black
30. Jacob – I will call boy
31. Lamont – daddy's home. I'm telling.
32. Malachi – baby blue (moving)
33. Maverick – black (moving)
34. Antonio – red and black checkered
35. Collin – orange, that personal interview
36. Jeremy – beige two piece. Do you mind
37. Craig – green – party. I ain't even mad
38. Pierce – run it boy
39. Kevin – that interview, the closet
40. Sean – stay the night
41. Warner – take you up and down
42. Charleston – No Limit

Our last name is Nelson.

4+3 = 7
Flawless.

12/25/19 I will be 7 y ears old.

Abigail Joyce.

Nickel Nicole. Los Nietos.

It's all in here Shona.

Bad comes. Mal – colm.

Spanish.

Ja –Bad - Mal.

Warner – Warn our brothers.
Warning.

Emergency Room.

345 is the DO IT BIG number.

Their enemies had pain in them and was taking that out on them. Their prey. Who already had the enemy's permanent pain. Then they had to deal with the others pain on top of that.

Getting here to find this bullshit out. It hurts. It's 5:12PM 8/15/19.

Pizza. Peace.

You'll hear things, then you'll see them.

Perfect robots.

Arbor Vitae.

R – B Ro. Music.

The Periodic Table

11 Sodium

13 Aluminum

30 Zinc

40 Zirconium

43 Technetium

45 Rhodium

The robots and settings will tell me everything I need to know to write the number ones. What happened to the world? God's precious creations.

Is there a board? To this game.

Signs told me not to.

Signs told me not to take that job. 221. 112. 290. 292. 117.

Public. Private.

Sign out front of the storage had my birthday on it. It was a church address or something and I went and the church wasn't there. It didn't exist. Rosecrans.

 This game is tough.

Took it out of my brain. Now I have to do all these damn puzzles to clamp it back in.

This is about freeing people. One life to live. 40.

Something's missing with the clamp.

Breaking point until watch what I need to.

Only let out of cages at certain times. Chained around the neck, feet and arms. And put in cages. Cells.

Breaking point to watch what I need to.

I feel like I have no one.

Pain unbearable.

Constant pain. 10-24-22.

Too many animals down there.

Mixtures. Half human, half animal. Half shit we could never imagine.

The streets. Attorney Weekends. Answer. Constant answers of yes and yet still this game, the rules won't complete. If I follow the rules, and have no money, I will feel defeated some way. But people need to be free.

People put in small spaces. Put in boxes. To cater to evil. Beasts and people.

The clamp.

It will hit hard. 4:17PM.

I'm the Momma! Screams. The bus that day. A bald big headed man that looked like the man I thought was God for a while. I met him by the bench. First words. Didn't understand. Second ones, got me to turn around. He had on a blue shirt. Which was a signature one for me with the man I thought was God for a while.

THE BOOKS.

THEY HAVE THE TRUTH.

Naturally written. The point: to save humanity.

They can be read and taken in an infinite amount of ways.

I said some trust that I know what's best.

But that robot said they're trying to lure me in.

Am I the only way out.

I have to stop adding to this.

I need to believe though that everything is written in here and in the 3rd installment of Connections.

It's the puzzle to free everyone once and for all. After that, everyone will be free and life goes on with what needs to go on.

Revenge.

I mean it.

I said this was to help me figure out all I want to do in life.

The present is a gift.

No pain.

These people get shit put in their eyes, vagina, ass holes, and penises.

They are cut.

Their chests get cut opened to see if they have hearts.

Cameras in eyes. So when sleep. It'll be like watching a movie in my head.

Bee snitches. These little things giving off sounds. Some maybe loud. Talking sounds.

Uh oh. Knowing more than one language. The animals.

No way.

Hell no.

This is what they want me and my family going through huh?

The real one.

This is it.

Legends.

Discipline.

This is it.

I need to start studying what I wrote.

The things the lady did to the woman who slept with her husband and was spending her money.

The things mother's did to boys that did their daughters wrong. Listening to their tears.

These people exist folks. They'll kill you or torture you in a second. If they hold a high job, they'll make you pay. Some are very evil. 44.

Weight. Let it burn. Cannot lose any if keep eating fast food. Once again, could've been done if I just would've stuck to the diet and dates I set. I already know how much I can lose. I've done it before. Now I have the weight back and will not eat as much or diet every other day when I lose it again.

Cannot get back to my superstar weight if I don't let it burn. Miserable every time I eat something outside of the fast.

Have a head start on looking good when the money comes.

These people are escorted out to mess with the beast. Food black mail. This story just keeps getting worse. I'm getting images though.

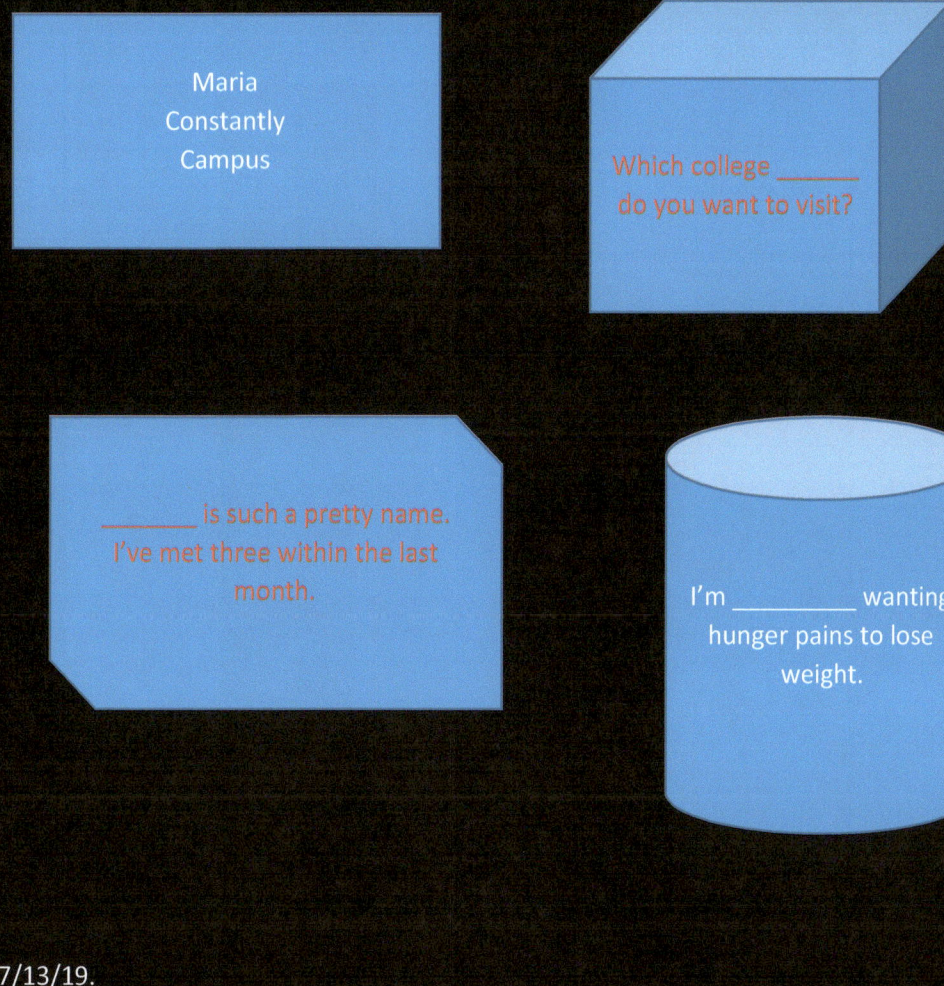

Maria
Constantly
Campus

Which college _____
do you want to visit?

_____ is such a pretty name.
I've met three within the last
month.

I'm _____ wanting
hunger pains to lose
weight.

7/13/19.

Real survivors.

They may not be at rock bottom.

Underground prisons.

Pet cemetery.

Flesh sucked out or what of dead bodies?

Coming to a land near you: HELL. The beast want to get above ground. They feel lied too. Different species. Many. Some are alone and playing stupid. How the fuck did this happen?

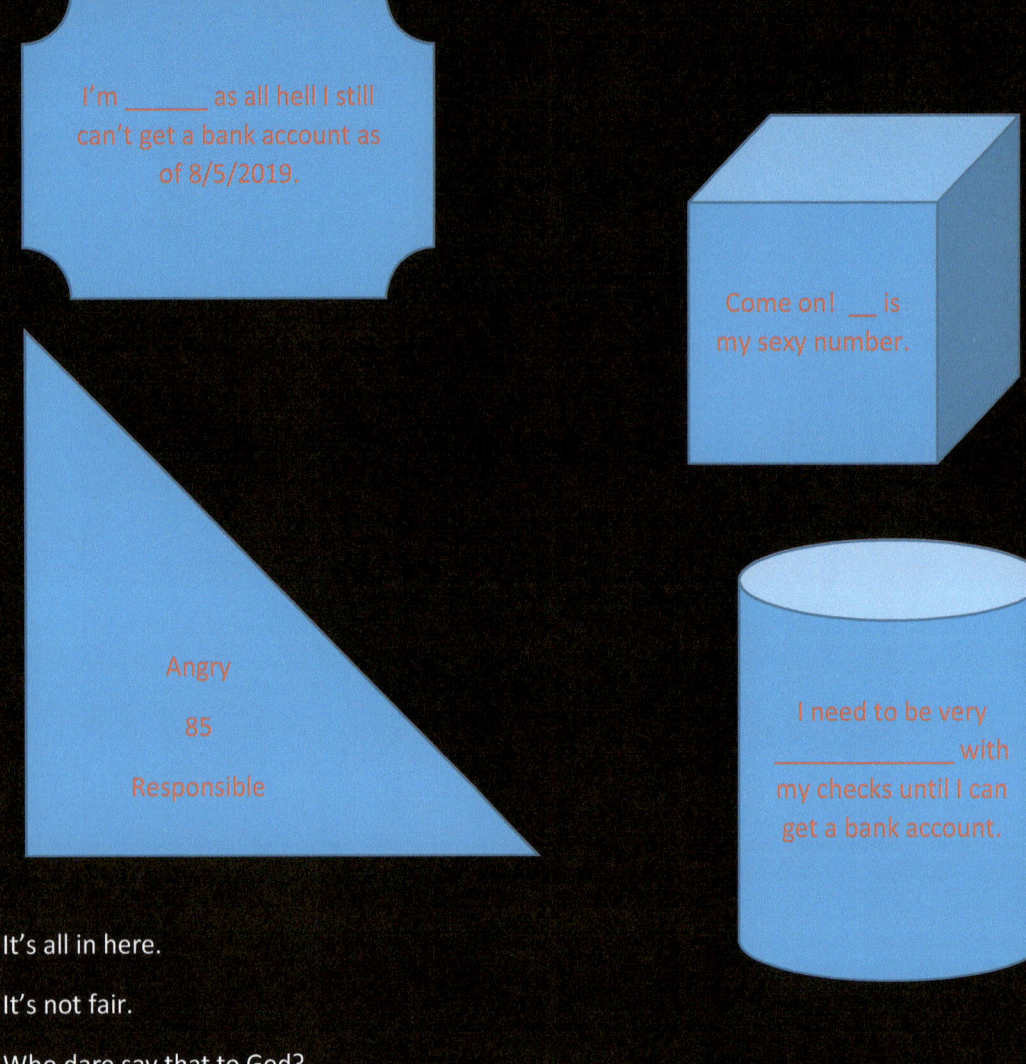

I'm _____ as all hell I still can't get a bank account as of 8/5/2019.

Come on! ___ is my sexy number.

Angry

85

Responsible

I need to be very _____ with my checks until I can get a bank account.

It's all in here.

It's not fair.

Who dare say that to God?

These people have to sleep in _____!

They have to sleep in things that don't allow them to _____.

Move
Boxes
They

_____have to argue with each other in an attempt to get the monster's attention to get out of being angry. Something like that.

About the weather and control of creations.

God cared none. He still lets them live.

Peasants.

Amateurs.

There is a guide to follow. Like it or not.

We're all playing this game.

The characters are trying to tell me what to watch, but no way to know.

She's too smart for that.

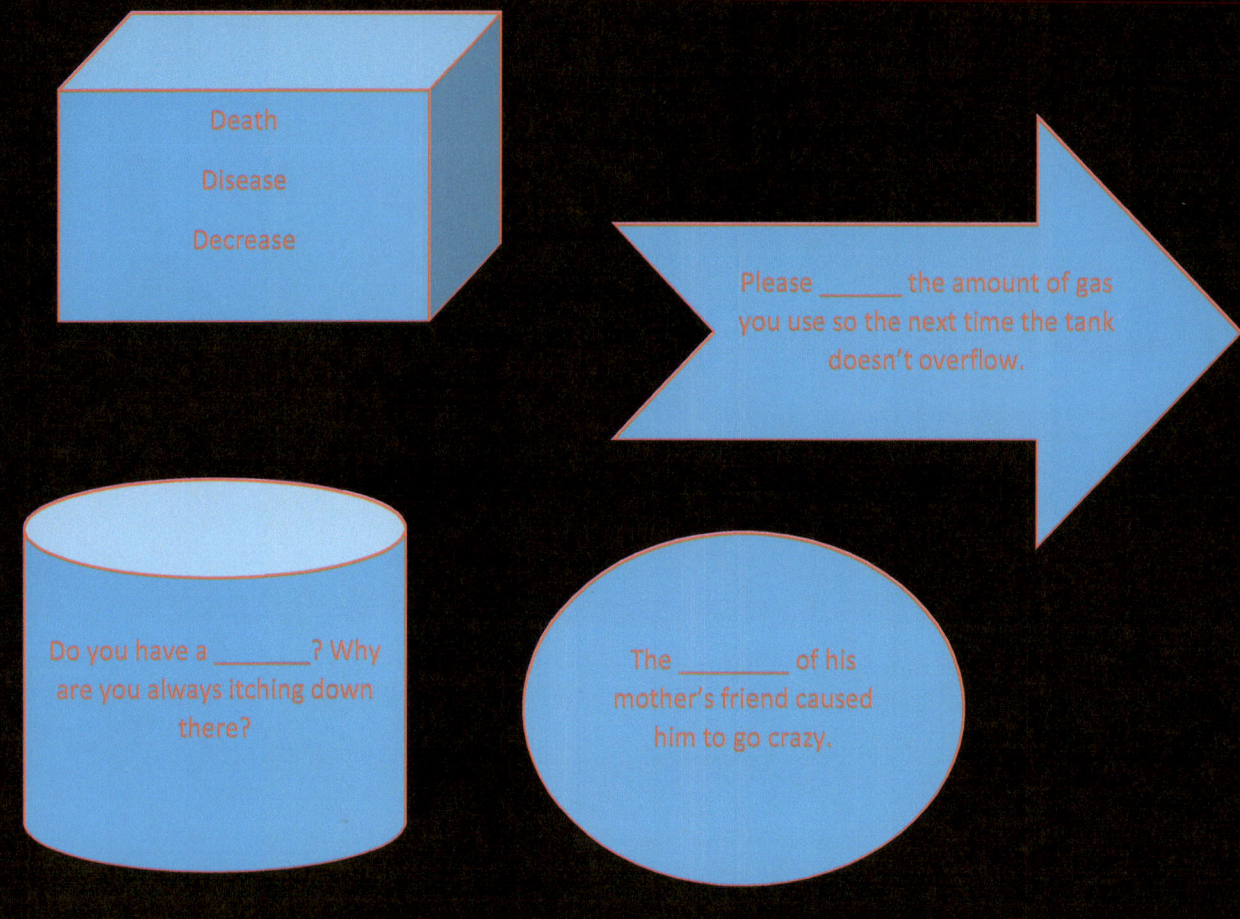

Death

Disease

Decrease

Please _____ the amount of gas you use so the next time the tank doesn't overflow.

Do you have a _____? Why are you always itching down there?

The _____ of his mother's friend caused him to go crazy.

Score. Scholar.

The books. Naturally written.

They're codes.

The codes unveil things.

Believe.

Things revealed. It's a real game of pretty jewels.

Some people are in animals. They want freedom bad again. They also want REVENGE.

I don't even think God knows how this happened.

I said He starred in a movie I made.

I said He starred in a movie that was made.

Olives

I'll live

All live

They _____ _____ happily
in their new home.

I love eating _____
like Noldar.

_____ _____ even
though I'm angry.

It's all in here.

I made a character and He hopped in him.

Still dealing with this up and down rollercoaster.

Family holding on to me.

Not letting her daughter, her baby, go that easy.

Never a day she wants me to go without knowing she's my mom.

And I have brothers.

This is a deadly game.

209. 2009. 29. The concert year. Her number in the line. The bus. The death year. The fight year.

2+9=11

1=1

EVEN.

Sores in their eyes.

Things with mouths on their foreheads.

Things talking with their feet.

Some things have more of one animalistic feature than others.

We're living in our last days. This shit is beyond me. Damn right it's the last days if all hell is going to come to Earth

Comm

Or

Con

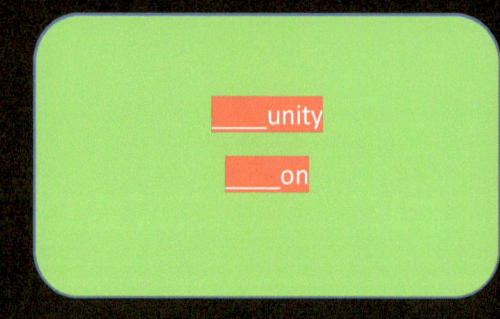

____unity

____on

How can you be drugged, still know what you're doing, but can't control what you're doing? But in your right mind to feel the emotion as your regular self.

Drugged to do what they want you to do, and feel it as if you weren't drugged.

Now that evil girl from the dinner comes to mind. She's not on my nerves now. Just seems like someone that was showing she will show out when civilization, the underground comes back above ground.

One big hell party that will be under control.

The animalistic people will try again to be normal.

The motto: all of us will be trapped. No one's going up and leaving us here.

Now they need answers to know who to torture the most.

But because they don't know, they torture everyone.

The clamp. Real! They got them.

But they are still trapped in cages.

Left for dead.

I think not!

Everyone's down there.

Real inventors and smarts left down there. The animalistic people were not free.

Their animalistic people left above ground have been killed.

They're waiting on signals, but there are none.

My robots killed them or family.
And now our crew is walking around.

What exactly is going to take place up here?

I'll learn soon.

We'll learn soon.

Hall of Win!

Misuse

Misinterpreted

You _____ what I said and that's why you're angry. I love kids. Just not yours.

Pure Hell down there. No chance of saying anything good.

They do dirty things to try and get the beast back.

They dress as their kids to get back people that are bothering them.

They get to new territory dressing as animals.

People dying. Only machine people. Robots. Right in their faces, the beast, and they don't know.

Human kind not as stupid as they think.

Payback. Their mind is set on revenge.

Help is on the way.

They know the upper ground has been switched.

Now they have to do their part beneath the ground.

Some have to shoot themselves every day. Helping each other.

It's going down when they get above ground. They will walk right out and right into new territory.

The land, 3:14pm, it will be, wait.

It's 7/11/19.

That's seven days a week. Even.

Pictures.

Picture this.

This type of revenge. Talking to beasts.

Birds that talk. Made normal above ground. How?

Talking animals with things registered in them about humanity's sanity and what it takes to make them click.

All clipped. All chipped. The animals. Above ground.

Who created what? I'll wait.

Humans and animals.

Just think.

Well. Maybe that's how you got beneath the ground in the first place.

You gone do it again? Keep quiet? Not think out of the ordinary? Fine.

The first humans. They know the truth. Or maybe they don't. It's not fair that He can do anything.

People talking of death and ruining holidays and all sorts of things on purpose.

ON PURPOSE!

These psychological things that play over in people's minds.
These games that play over in people's minds.

I had to watch, visualize the events at that restaurant over and over to get the question I needed answered. The right question will get the first response or something like that. No. Infinite answers.

Looking evil at people will get you evil reactions from them.

Their homes invaded with cameras. By all types of people. Including ones they went to school with. All their sex activities, personal conversations. Recorded. They wronged too many people to know who did it.

They got played by people that weren't for their sorry ways. Some were their friends.

They're still bitter and want to trick everyone into going under there.

Or are they aware that they need help and help is not beneath the ground with them?

I said some gave in and don't want their only chance of escaping getting trapped.

I would rearrange these robots to get on my nerves and convince me of the worst with these people so that I could have everything I need written in this book.

All the things I've done.

Could've done less and had the money by now.

Then all of this crazy transforming shit would be for nothing.

I don't need this.

King

Sing

Ring

Thin____

Ris_____

Ri____

Bles____

I want to be thin. Fast food bloats my stomach. Takes too long to digest.

To drugs. It's a new day. Drugs will help these people because they have illnesses far greater than the drugs side effects. Some type of brain shit like that. Things that work that are never spoken of.

Accidents reviving people. Huh? The first drugs. The first prisons. Hostages. Truth or not. It's just a book.

Now I know what people that are overweight feel like.

They want everything and to get out.

Sit around and wait on me. Some work on escape.

Snobby people caught.

Oh brother.

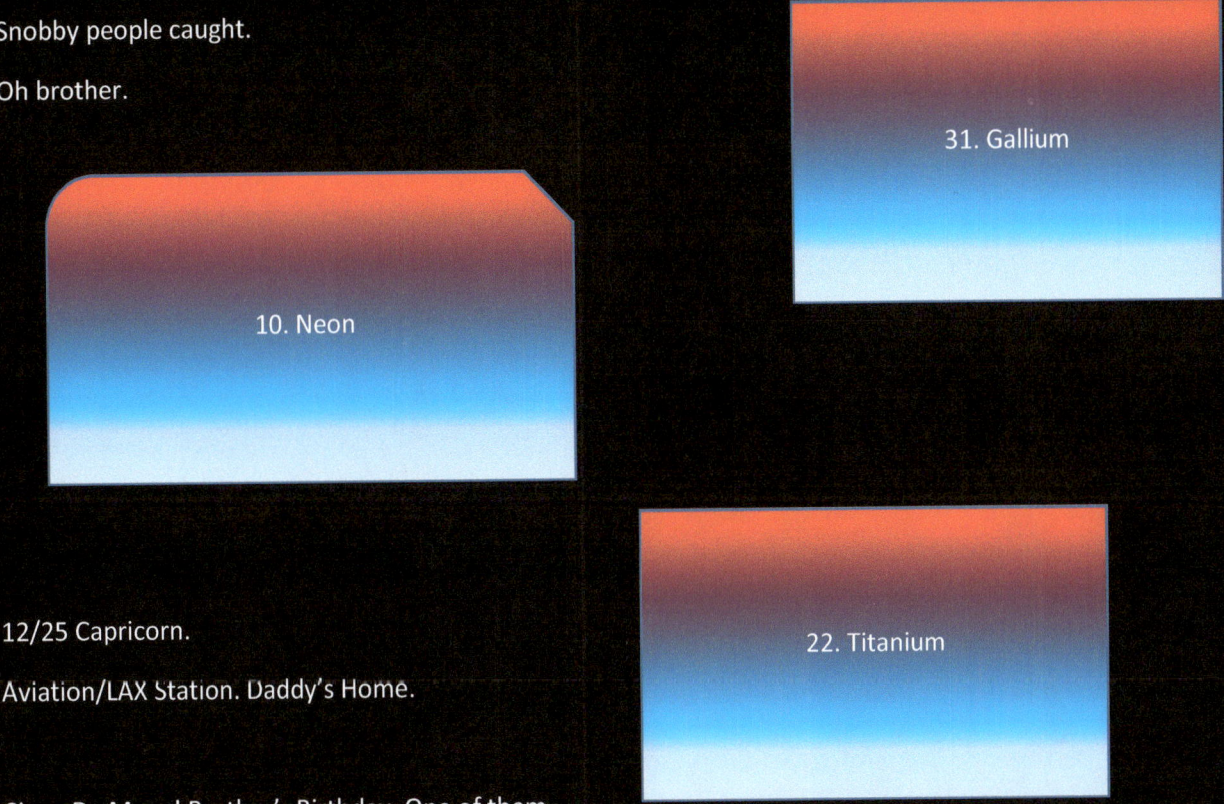

31. Gallium

10. Neon

22. Titanium

12/25 Capricorn.

Aviation/LAX Station. Daddy's Home.

There's no way the last people could know about all of them and their past.

All of family is here watching me.

Only natural foods. (Then everyone would be in shape)

Some foods are made of terrible things.

Faces above ground. Lies planted. One of the greatest minds ever. All the games they play. No confirmation they're alive.

Said I need the platform to figure out how I made everything.

I feel like my body is unbalanced.

I just can't believe it got this bad.

 I mean these people have fake teeth in their mouths and the skin on their private areas isn't theirs. They were left for dead and made it. Well, some of them.

But I still can't get a grip, grasp on if they are alive or not.

Kept in cages is where they belong.

They have us worrying about shit that hasn't happened and most likely won't, and they say it's us with the issue since we let them bother us. They think they not doing nothing and they know they are.

Complete trash.

We already can't believe they exist.

The Point: my younger self has prepared a good way for my older self.

Need to be patient. Perfect arrival.

Someone's height changes over night and you/no one wants to talk about it.

Some people with diseases crack. Meaning they go on a killing hunt.

Mixing things /sentences up in this writing and it will click and match when I read it.

Coded. Much.

Well it's all in here.

At the end of the day, I'm still here. Things to do. There's good food. I don't need to have kids. Me and my robots can enjoy ourselves.

Although humanity's infested with stuff. Homeless or not.

They may not be at rock bottom.

Songs reminding me of what's happened in the past. Robots. Some kind of way. The machine. It works.

They're in cages.

Animals adjust to how they walk. Adjust to how they talk. The humans make up its genes. Genetic makeup. Wait is that right to say?

They act crazy to distract animals.

Take punishment.

Reminder: No nice sentences allowed.

They talk in all types of ways to let their loved ones know they love them.

All hell all day long.

The real slaves.

The Real Slaves.

These people always see the evil people they don't like did. Literally right in front of them. Their faces. As if they're really there. The explosion: the beginning of the false Information Age.

It's like they're constantly being beaten up. I'm going through all this shit. Experiencing all these diseases. In – Form – A – Tion.

I made these robots. The fine ones will come around.

The Story and Projections, expansion on what happened here.

I made it.

My stomach literally turned. Like a blood, heavy blood ball was in it. These people are that annoying.

They can't raise kids.

They let them do whatever they want.

The shit monsters think they are light.

My brother face painted a girl with care to show me how much he loves me. It's what we have to do.

For now. I can't believe I'm related to these men. I love them to death and would do anything for them.

Who started the trend it's good to be messy and gossip all the time?

Who told women that shit was cool?

Is that really what these men want? Is it really what they classify as a bad bitch?

Looks, has issues and needs to gossip, nice hair, attitude when things don't go her way.

That's what a man wants in a woman?

Drama is good?

Lying ass kids with no discipline?

Paid in full I said.

I can't believe my stomach turned, these mutha fuckas are that annoying.

They don't raise their kids or don't know how and they keep having more.

This type of shit. Have to have a kid, kill it, then eat it and they're still not happy.

7/13/19.

This is a love so deep.

We can touch each other with just looking at each other.

Men forced to wear pads with blood. This shit is beyond me.

I feel like someone's pulling strings in my head.

This is a brain.

Yes talking about committing suicide all the time can make you want to commit suicide.

Let people keep arguing for nothing.

Doing wrong and it's on tape you and your daughter/son know that you were wrong and laugh about it and don't care.

I have always been brought out of suicide by these robots.

Learned things the hard way over time. The second time. Next time around I'll be smarter.

I don't know if they're separated or not.

Now every day I wake up I'm suicidal.

I said my creations meant nothing to them. They're in pain.

The Real Slaves.

True Survivors.

A wave is coming to a land near you.

We'll be ready.

We'll put it right in your face.

Chipped people.

Ones with the worst things chipped in the beast, have to get tortured a lot.

The beasts have connects to get information from other places.

The game of phones.

Person to person. Animal to animal.

They're in cages.

Telephone.

More lies spread.

But the positive is these robots have kept me alive. Why I can't make up my mind or get the confirmation on who my real family is, is beyond me. I do know I wanted to experience all the hell that these people are dealing with or have dealt with during their time in hell from humans.

I'm currently homeless. I have to carry all of my things with me to the job I just got. I have no friends.

I just can't wait to get back on my feet.

Considering the headache they give, is it worth it?

It's starting to kill me to think that they're captured and not where they belong.

Yes. Every morning, even people good to you become annoying in your thoughts.

These people are playing a game of suicide. Have to shoot their whole family for a bite of something to eat sometimes.

2 times.

Need to remember my robots are causing hell to people I hate too.

People, experts, trying to make people commit suicide. (mechanisms, mannerisms)

Time to move forward and edit.

My only way to remain out of suicide is to continue on with the books.

It's mandatory to free humanity. If you have the talent to do so. Talent sounds fun. Skill. Ability.

Does God care if humanity is freed?

I think not. They shouldn't have gotten in that space, place in the beginning.

How cool is that to have live visuals of what is going on?

Legends.

The books are what is needed to hop out of suicide faster. I need more of the story. Then the images will project.

These people were forced to have babies and eat them alive.

They're that annoying they make you sick to your stomach. Miscarriages caused because of them.

My family is furious. They have to show me what they wish they were doing to me and all the things we used to do.

This is war.

These robots I said can do anything.

Transform from women to men. Human to beast. Machine to whatever is visible. Ghosts.

I'm furious at this up and down suicide battle.

I'm adjusting the robots so I can get a harsh, the fullest of what they're experiencing, what I'm supposed to be experiencing. In that hell hole.

Of what happened.

Her name. It naturally was said by that deep voiced woman when I read it. It happened more than once.

My mind knows it's there.

There's a computer in me.

It's time to celebrate not adding any more to this story. This book. 2:03pm. 2:04pm.

That's what it is.

Legends.

Sorry ass boring ass people want to be friends with cool people and they fuck shit up. They're boring, no personality and only can hold conversations about gossip.

Monster's with a bunch of eyes.

I keep saying these people have paid in full for what they've done and what they are like, and who they've become.

But the fact remains they would have never changed if they didn't get they ass beat and they should have naturally changed their ways or never been like that in the first place.

I mean all this sorry ass shit, these people deserve to go.

They can stay.

They go from station to station.

Only way to get over them is to not think about them.

Every day I wake up I'm unsure if my family is my family, but a little closer to clamping it in.

They're down there playing a damn game of suicide.

I need to remember if I'm down there, my robots are causing hell to the people I hate too.

They're in cages.

There are some people down there that are cool. Those are the ones I let hop in my 'hologram' bodies. The explosion is why stories of saying sorry when you're about to die and that false place of heaven exist.

No one else.

People, anyone hopping in your bad thoughts and saying the worst of the worst. It's real sharp.

That's every person you see, reacting to you in a way you don't like whether they do something good or bad. Have done bad or good to you.

I mean it.

Someone had a shaved face one day, and the next day a beard. And ya'll thought it was the same person.

The hell is wrong with you?

I mean, look at all these sorry ass people. I need to figure out how to get that invisible revenge.

Hearing a cough assuming it's someone and they didn't see his or her face. So getting mad and finding a way to piss that person off that they think it was. These people were trash. Always have been.

Monsters unbelievable. Some of their faces look like a bunch of black eyed peas combined making up their face or whole bodies.

There's things having babies out of their heads, ass, back. All types of places. I mean it. People make jokes about people with large families. A lot of siblings. Mom's getting it in. Theirs is getting it in too/she probably just getting abortions.

Eating live bodies. Spiders.

Mansions, cars all types of expensive shit left to beasts. Since when, the beginning? Nobody thought of a way to fix that shit.

Scared they'll never experience a good life with their family again. I can see the inside of me filled with grey circles.

I said I was curing them of diseases every day/daily. This type of insanity.

No way. The eyes. It's the eyes.

I always said you shouldn't drink shit from an animal.

How the hell can this be?

Never heard of this shit.

Something has to be wrong.

Eating things alive and the shit still lives inside of them and they spit it out if they can or shit it out.

Swallowing it whole really backfires. They have to please the beast. But it knows the truth.

125.

323.

213.

504.

Do to Ron Me.

The evil dialogue gets faster.
I mean it; they clashed. All types of fuckery and combined they put together why they were going insane. Being around people like their family drives them more crazy. How insane is that? Kill worthy?

I have to stay busy to hop out of suicide.

Crazy people around more crazy people will make them crazier. They need sane people to help them snap out of chaos. Chaotic thoughts.

If you see someone that's not there and she sees someone else that's not there and ya'll are responding to them in front of each other, something terrible can happen to your brains.

All types of shit we know is wrong, or maybe we don't, and we do it anyways.

To keep less space. Way more mental illnesses, diseases than the ones listed in books. Taught in schools.

To not take up so much space.

All types of shit the beasts figured out was wrong that people did to them and don't think humans will ever know. The beasts think the humans are stupid. The humans play mentally ill now.

Walking beasts above ground again. Torture. Real fuckery coming soon. In ways no one will know.

Brothers.

Mommy and Me.

LynWood

The Study Guide!

It's all in here.

It's all right here.

Hard annoyances from robots to snap me back into reality. Annoyance as a way to snap out of a bad trance and into a regular nice person. These types of pained illnesses. All out revenge these people will be out for. They won't sleep well until they get it. Developed crews/armies in.

Forced to do everything to everyone's face. The things they said and did behind their backs and these people got to fight them and harm them for what they did. All out revenge and fuckery.

A huge storm is coming this way. 43.

Are they putting their eyes in the robots? Or me. Or when I think of them, it (their eyes can be put in the robots) convenient who I see first, think about. Gas.

Drill it in. Everything else not written has already been made. Everything will be revealed.

The musician. Projects already done. Stick to the plan. Braid hair. Grease. Park.

The beast doesn't like to be black. Gets them free time.

Videos get them free time. The man sitting on the car stop waiting on his visit from hell.

The Cult. The two homeless girls that met on the bus and became lovers.

They will want to know everything that's happened to them. Shona, you can't write everything.

The Guide. Commercials playing at the right time. I said they wouldn't just let them out of their cell. Captivity for a few seconds to do these clips.
I also said they had to search and find them in their cells, cages.

The table. The dorms. % The tree. Capitol. Books.

The only way out of their cell is to act disgusting. Realize and feel better.

All of my family is here and watching.

Experiencing the headache these people gave/give people and are forced to experience and on a worse level. Fucked by people they said they never wanted to touch. Forced to lie to them and say they like them or are in love with them. This type of evil so they can cum. Come where?

All the games they play, no one knows if they are alive. No confirmation they're alive. One of the greatest minds. Lies planted. I don't know these people. Family separated early. I feel like my body is unbalanced. 10-23-22. 10-25-22. 10-31-22. 11-1-22. 12-3-22.

They have to dress as beast to work on the escape.

Which event.

The point. To be able to see new things happen and my heart not stop for a few seconds or be effected.

504 is an area code. So that's a little something concerning the 45 of us. These signs will be all over. These people will never go a day without thinking of me and my family. And every second I think they don't, they gone pay. They think they are the best evil people.

Ya'll know some of these people are shaped weird. Have huge heads. Are just ridiculous in height. Too tall. Damn near the size of the basketball rim, and ya'll gone walk around and not say shit because of what?

I mean. These shit monster people have annoying voices and don't take no shit. They could care less. Their heart doesn't budge. DISCIPLINE. DISCIPLINE. DISCIPLINE!!! IS ALL THEY KNOW. DO IT RIGHT THE FIRST TIME. WHY DO YOU NEED INSTRUCTIONS? SHIT.

I said these people would come above ground. Everyone free. And it will just be a complete war zone.

I look out the window like my robots don't know my peripheral can see them or I can see them through the window and they answer me with a head movement. Like yea. Duh. We know you are looking at us.

Trying to hit that forty five.

Trying to clamp who la familia is.

Ella can.

I mean it! How the hell did these things get teeth, voices? I mean the dump these shit monsters came out of is unbelievable. A combination that never stopped. Who the hell? The first people. What the fuck? Where exactly does the trash go? Metal mixed with shit and dead bodies. They have teeth don't they. They grow like us. They can reproduce. How the hell? It's all happened.

I can't believe this shit.

Brothers, Mommy, Me and Daddy.

This will work. Keep reading it and things will be pieced together.

1.   Have to travel to different parts of. Stay here. Thoughts. Platform.

2.   Watch different videos.

3.   Platform if I feel like it. (Family trying to get me to realize I'm bigger and have created things bigger than what I know) (Far beyond average intelligence)

4.   Puzzles. They will tell me what to watch and help me clamp in the truth.

It's all in here. 1,2,3.

I feel healthy.

Gets them free time.

The table.

Movie. Blood. Jo- why – See.

Video games.

That room. They're hiding from the beasts. Using the weak. No one. Bricks. Stone. Circles.

Circles and Bricks.

Legends.

Do to Ron, Me.

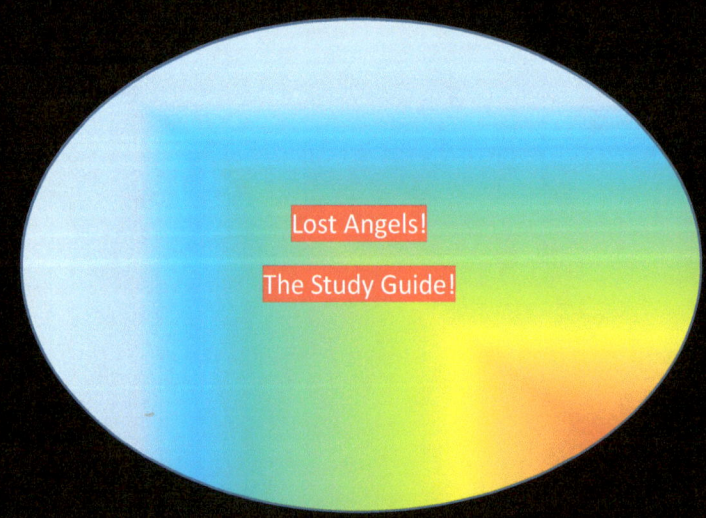

To hear outside of me. That place at the mall. I said she heard my thoughts. They were smart. It was a robot of me.

They can die any day down there. Parents trying to keep their kids alive. These parents.

Surely if I can chip, clip them all, projections are showing.

Rewiring my brain so I can go down there naturally. Visit the underground, that is.

Then all of this was for nothing. We'll tell them who we are.

Same thing, but better.

Mad as hell.

Hearing what you're thinking or who you see.

Look alike robots saying, asking you have you seen a movie of the person they really look like.

Ghost town. 10 years plus some of these people have been trying to keep their kids alive.

Can speed time up and won't even know. Shot in my brain. My medicine. I did things in theirs too.

Supposed to watch family and that popstar every day.

The thing is, this is a gift. I'm supposed to enjoy looking at many different rooms at once. Just not respond to them. In public. Or when I'm with another person/group etcetera.

That thought that the robots keep intercepting before I can figure out what it is. Coincidence?

His voice is so mesmerizing. Things, extremes I'd go through to save him. I can't believe he's supposed to be my brother. Too good to be true.

Ok. Stick to the script.

And you end up in here. Surrendered to white masters. Beasts. Votes. I think it's: are you mine? Are you alive? Are they going through complete hell?

Trapped. Used to the smell. It answers them all at once. Getting used to the smell. Parents forced to say they don't want their kids. It was painful. Having them.

The devil. Lived. Evil lives. These girls: If I can't have you, then I will cause you complete hell.

See it backwards?

Hoes Would!

The Study Guide!

These were their partners. Have to do something for the beasts. Get it supplies. Food. Show up.

Are robots down there?

Unbelievable things going on down there.
Am I able to shake the place and give them food, clothes, hope? Is there a route for the escape?

Mom is bitter too. Her daughter, the only one, going through this shit.

Who family is will be revealed naturally.

Think positive. Be positive. Be confident.

Surely I could save my mom and family if they were down there.

It hurts like hell these robots just don't cater to me and bow down. I made them. They do what's best for me. They're like parents. So that's the right way to make them.

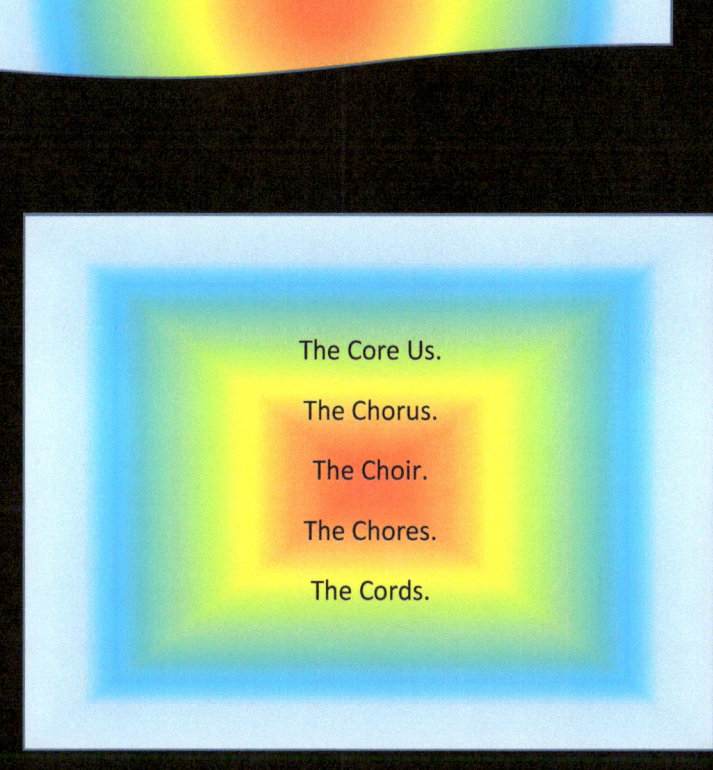

Say it Loud!

The Core Us.

The Chorus.

The Choir.

The Chores.

The Cords.

I shut down. Brain. And didn't even know. Said would be world wars and people were related to me that weren't. Oh, it was to tell me that even these rude ass people's relatives don't like them. Talking about the less fortunate, not cool.

24 hour surveillance. Harmed to steal something and hit it. Experimented until I found something that worked. Harmed to steal something and hide it. Said they couldn't wait for me to show up.

The 4 year old boy. Mistreated. A dose of more of their annoyance. Constantly. Robots telling me the story. The last ones above land. Chained around the neck. No movement. Still breathing.

The language.

If not, robots will be cool. I can make a nice looking and nice in general people.

These people would not care if I was trapped. They don't know me. Enjoy my life.

They'll move naturally and I won't see it. Drugs falling to help them drug beasts. It's all in here. Will be writing all day. Chipped. It's in their bones. Robots. The animals so big they can't stand. Some animals without legs naturally created. Want to learn the language.

Always worrying about negative shit because of these muh fuckers. Every morning ruined. Like someone stealing my papers and they're not even in this state. These gnats. Drill it in. They've paid in full for every annoyance they've done.

14 hours.

Without this money I'm bitter.

I can make myself feel like these people. I was walking to the train station and (it's 10:22AM) I felt like that boy that I think is my brother, walking. Hopeless.

Consolidated spaces. Claustrophobic and squished. Separated. Force out negative thoughts. Gain a new attention. Desperation for help. Anything. God would want you to be smart and carry on. God is the realist. Be thankful to be breathing.

Be thankful and smart.

I immediately saw a problem and experimented until I found something that worked.

I feel like if all the players, humankind died and nothing was left but beast, God would just start over. No heart attacks. We wouldn't know.

These annoying people. They have a lie for every way you answer a question. It's trash. Punishment. They paid in full. Their faces lit completely on fire and some made it. Unbelievable. Slave Situations.

Fire on back. Hit on back. (rock on pebble) hit my brain. Hexagon. Sight of her. This training.

I said evil was better than them in a sense they weren't that annoying but they're killers. The straight way, go right to you and just give you pain so they're not. The trash though, killers with annoyance. Takes a while.

Convincing your mind. Hear it too many times. People take for granted how powerful what they put in their brain is or don't think about it.

The Disappearing Act. Of humankind and humanity. Person by person. Group by group.

State by state. Country by country. Continent by continent.

Everything will play out in front of me.

Without anything, should still help these people. Whether sleeping on the bench or bus, or apartment.

The point.

If these people are gone, it's probably best I am outside. Too much information to be crammed inside.

They can't believe someone would take their lives because of their fuckery. Not kill them. Just freedom. When projected they still have to act like they hate their family and explain their ways that people don't like; these people are talked about to the max. Have/had to talk about people they love here.

Slavery passed down. It's in their blood.

Icons.

Legends.

Surrounded by many people and talked about.

I said the last ones could've saved the place with their knowledge, but too focused on their sex appeal and making people ache because they can't sleep with them.

All they do is talk about people.

I can't believe I'm up here trying to figure out who my family is.

It's all right here.

It's all in here. No common sense. Learned things the hard way.

Heart rate. I have to do it. It'll all play out in front of me or behind me. Wherever projected. I can see. It. Keep doing puzzles. Puzzles tell me what to watch. Still trying to clamp for sure that they are alive. And can see projections. Money and family.

Uh oh. Just had an upward sprout. Meaning dose of I'll make it to tomorrow. With more information. That's the real way. Everything's good. All the drama, computerized things, lies, mess, poverty, wannabes.

These robots. They have babies. They bleed. Reproduce blood.

I see my younger self pop out of these robots and now her head is moving with a pen or. And now her hand is moving with a pen or marker and poster board.

Someone created. Huh? Place. It's a damn shame. But he does exist. But it is made up. It's a damn shame. Man made every. Each book of it. Huh? Some.

All of this to wake up to this. Still have to play dumb with my own robots. Why homeless?

Army demons coming when free but robots will have it under control.

These robots are trying to tell me something?

All hell on Earth? Hmm. Demons. My robots snapping at me. It's on and poppin' around here. Real Soon.

My younger self is trying to tell me something.

You look at your phone then up and that person is there. Scare tactics. The way a word is said triggering your heart. You never know how to take it. You ponder on it all day. You react to it many ways.

You look anywhere. Clothes following you around.

It's some crazy ass shit going on around here. All frauds will be replaced.
The replacements coming soon.

I know one thing, all this up and down with my heart. This constant feel of suicide, these people are dead, well will feel like it. Blood.

Blood needs to be shed. They would do it to us and are doing it now. They would do it to us. With no emotion but arousal in their privates.

The lab. How synthetic things were made. The locations. Not knowing who my family is has me hot.

But I stand by my word. Why would I not give them the fame?

Real bullshit. People couldn't just enjoy life. Had to throw in I look better than you, have more money, then more siblings. Damn. Bragging for what? Poison. That's what it is though huh?

Understand she's trying to hug and say she loves me, my mom, by people walking by. My brothers too.

Stick to the plan. Career and will get more answers.

Having to play all types of ways. Responses. Lies and I want to tell the truth but can't. My own creations getting on my nerves.

They're putting shit over their eyes so they can't see the projections.

I said they were counting their footsteps.

This money system. Real. This shit. Hurts. Small ways and inch by inch, decimal by decimal to get free. Every second counts. 10:43AM.

Real. Takes a lot for them to get out. I need to sing. All this and their pain. Now things above ground. They want out. I will feel better when I complete a piece of the game. Things hurt. Have to free them.

Slow songs written. Created too much. Under estimate me. New names.

Slavery still. I knew they wouldn't stop and lied to their kids about other races being evil first.

Brains full of things people say to them and the reactions naturally coming out. Or they think it's cute. Older people being treated young (maybe by boyfriend). And it comes out in public. Ways you act behind closed doors constantly. Then you get mad when you do them in public. This is a mind.

Someone can do all of this and still be suicidal. Dealing with these fucked up people.

I said they had to create rooms with people they liked and didn't like to be good and bad and cater to the beast. Even it's peripheral.

I'd be writing all day. I will sense all negative things and my thoughts will become negative.

It's me these robots keep saying. The one to save the world. But not him. I'm not him. Gifted. Ants all over. And I'm putting myself through pain to come to all types of realizations.

Student first. Once it clicks, clamps they're alive or why I put myself through this, I can move on or go back to the platform.

Step by step I have to take this. And day by day. Need to remember that I'm still learning things at a steady pace. My thoughts will become negative if I don't keep up with the game.

Are they helping? Can they help down there? Or are my robots doing all the work? People taking in beast costumes. Skin.

The cost and goods. The holograms cost. These inventions. By me. Don't believe.

They're dead. Except us. Compare how good holograms are to the pain a human can suffer.

Yes I would, so they can live. What is the question? It was down there.

I said there's no way to survive all that shit in your brain.

All the people they saw. Now I see myself projected walking by.

Ma. Real. Devil.

Downward spiral. Feel hopeless a little again.

Momma had some fine boys.

Wild animals. Sold as sex slaves too. I mean it. I don't even know them. Worldwide annoyances.

Different parties own different parts of the underground.

Visions. Will show me the truth.

Family has more controls than me.

Lots of fine men. Being on television. It's something about them.

Realize family can be in cages right now and in all types of pain right now.

Have to follow the system. Robots telling me. Hall of win.

Ma real. Devil.

This money system and all the different ways to locate me.

All the different ways to keep up with what I spend money on. I guess since thieves, we need this information. I mean, for others to have it.

Marinate in the things I have done. Why would it be for nothing? If anything, enjoy the place alone.

Things falling on their land, and they know they're being denied. The search for the rest of the goods.

The gift. Songs bringing up areas, reminding me of areas.

Clothes reminding me of places. Foods. Nouns.

No limit. Colors reminding me of a whole story I forgot. Built up thoughts.

Need to clamp in that these people are gone.

Then how?

Some of these families think I am a member of their family. Their sister. Brother.

Some crazy people see me, or another adult, and see a baby. How?

People that are over five feet are nowhere near a baby coming out the womb. These illnesses. You're looking right at us.

This cloud of suicide comes over me, then I snap out of it.

Is that what I do to them? I appear and show them many ways to believe they will be free?

Crazy out here folks.

Real insane people.

Out do the enemy.

Drugged. Some.

I can outdo the enemy.

Scare the enemy. I can scare their enemy and they don't.

A book system-ed, connected to the world.

Ways to know a robot is mine.

Forehead may shift and tell me who it is.

Infinite ways to know if a robot is mine.

Clamp in that these people are gone.

They lured more people beneath. Forced to by beasts. As well as slave masters.

When new recruits came, the older ones were killed and the newbies were forced to get new people.

It was made sure the older ones lured everyone they knew beneath the ground, before being killed.

The system designed to make you fail. They trying to kill us all. Money.

Color included. All types of tactics used to make people want to follow these people. Get them alone, which was a set up as well. Color of skin. Using that darker versus lighter tactic. By means of getting on people's nerves.

10:45AM. Game Over.

They got their asses beat and chipped inside, then led more people to the underground. 10:21AM.

This bitterness. Do as you're told or die. As well as them already not caring. 10:22AM.

Who the hell is my family?

Am I an only child?

It knows I'm getting closer and the right combination anywhere from any source adjusts so I can get the answer I need. They KNOW. Be in the know.

Feeling like holding on because of Mom. She gave me this life, then I have an episode where I don't know who my mom is. Meaning I have nothing to fall on and can go over on the deep end.

They can feel me being out of it. Suicidal. My family.

I mean it. I said I would never go off on the deep end.

Need to get even.

They're trying to kill us all is what was said. 168. Market. The combination: 6, 32, 18.

Back to the lab.

A whole system of people replaced by animals.

These mutha fuckas wanted the whole world for themselves. Everyone beneath the Earth unless working that day for them. I said this. Well some of it a while ago.

I feel like I've been everywhere because my robots are everywhere. Recording.

The writings. My brain already knows it's there. It's the machine.It's the eyes.

Puzzles, write, then throw away.

Juggling between families. This is bullshit.
Sex and watching them suffer, these evil bastards that want me and my family, if that's what it is then fuck it.

This suicide rollercoaster can kiss my ass. Meet Market. Meet at the market. Meet. We will meet. Mark it. Mark the date.

Bottom line, I've done too much not to enjoy it. Reconstructed, shots to the brain to alter my age. All of this for nothing and my younger self teasing my older self. No. something deeps there.

Wait. The prison. The red dress took over. It was the last to capture the whole building. I believe. Cages.

Drive. Up and down from feeling sorry for these people.

They still hold onto it's impossible for everyone to be down there and someone's being evil not helping them. And these particular ones weren't good for shit.

How? All the fuckery and no attention or joining together to figure out how to beat it. No one could do it. She's the only one. Fruit Delle. Stay Sean. Award Money.

I'm here. The family is too. There's nothing and no one anywhere else and I have to act like there is.

Time to figure out the truth and building my career is the study guide.

Words will clamp.

Billions.

I heard that lady shout the name of my character. My mind knows it's in the writing. It's there.

Silly of us to think slavery ended with some damn paper work.

I said they wouldn't let them out.

Shit people need to hear testimonies of instead of believing.

I can shoot things in their brains too.

Like they already did it.

23 is my Devil number. Evil. Ding Ding Ding. Bells!

See why? Money what? End End El. Elle. Z dash – En. End. Eat. Buffets.

Wash nigga ton.

Who would believe that?

Seasoning for the fast.

I'm just a lunatic. Right. Write. Directions. Color. Correct.

The books are all in me some kind of way. My clones wrote them. My mind's advanced.

Foods making your body let go of sounds you can't believe. This embarrassment.

How do you allow these to be made? Or did you already have some and they took over? The beasts.

Underground prisons. Caged up.

Having to strip and perform sexual favors for beasts.

This is beyond me. This is what the fuck they want to do to me.

I don't think they understand the type of chip I have naturally embedded in me taking me to suicide until I get all the facts.

Look at it like not being able to eat until you finish your chores for the day.

I need the full story. 3:47PM. This will hit.

It's already written. Things will adjust.

A war down there. Up here too.

They have to say terrible things and make them mean good things to their family with gestures.

No good words allowed. They're always listening. The beasts.

It's all in here.

Underground prisons. Caged up.
Trust.

I'm so fucking done. I forgot to add these beasts can make themselves look just like a particular human.
It's already in me like a death chip: learn the story or all things will be negative to you. You won't jump though. These robots I've created are flawless. They will arrange in a way so that I am sustainable, although negativity overtakes me, and still get me to do the proper task.

What type of fucking disastrous place of trash, electronics included, could allow something to be created that can change into real human form and real people and talk and have its voice.

And make more of it?

They have to stand in awkward positions that strain their bodies.

I mean all the hell they cause and for nothing or because someone else did something to them.

It's time to study for real.

With or without them, life goes on. It has to.

Legends.

There's no way they could escape without this technology.

Lunch tables.
The ones at that school were the same as his bed sheets. Also this lady's bag at work. G – Low Answer.
Answer Ro. L G.

When the tables fold up, the three blues. Or two blues. They were the same design and color tones as his bed sheet. Blanket. How crazy is that? This is too much. The purse.

I just want to eat all day and sleep.

These people have to stand in awkward positions.

I need this info here because I have to help save these people and they give me a headache in ways too.

Money.

Legends.

This shit hits.

All this suicide, I need some understanding.
How can you be black, and naturally degrade all black women except your mother?
Driving them to suicide and not giving a fuck? Yes I know other races have this issue. But blindly.
I need to know how to walk these robots to hell when they bother me. But it's just like this. It's a robot. It doesn't care. It's me reacting to me in a nasty way, and at the same time reacting in a way that the person the robot is will get annoyed. And the robots telling me a past story. And letting me know it's loyal.
The killing room.
The Killing Room.
The point: to control them live. My robots know far beyond what I do at the moment.
How does one make something like that? Toys! Human Toys! Everything's free! Supposed to be!

It needs to exist.

All types of devices I need to make. Learn to make.

Trust no one.

I'm trying to figure out who my family is with everything around me.

Snitches get stitches. Kiss my ass.

Games on a new level.

Who said it was 1 of every household that had many kids? Me or them?

There's a lot that's hard to believe.

Time out of cell.
Slavery.
I can hear her whisper. The Book!

Platform.

I need to understand why I shouldn't care if it's just me and robots.

Crazily, family puts me to sleep every night, so it's like I know they're here. Projections of them just walk up. And I'm not alone.
A party on the train. 3400 Avenue. Fireworks. Frisco. Bien. Good. A You. A ti. Crab Legs. Voila! Palm of my hand. Far. Ma. See Ya!

I can feel that people are alive beneath.

Getting back to that baby I was, and not caring about being alone. The pain I could be enduring. We, my family, could be enduring.

Enjoy the ride folks.

New words and phrases will come about as I do these puzzles and pay attention to the videos.

I can't get this show out of my head. It keeps expanding.

Thinking of things they project in your face.

We will just walk right in.

I said we will just walk right in the underground.

Practicing to make you want to commit suicide. These evil people with experience from their jobs.

The fight to just grasp that these people are alive.

Suicide creeping in me.

How the hell do I force their eyes in the computer?

The Cost.

This type of revenge. All you need is yourself and nothing or no one more. Even if I'm dead.

The more I watch a clip, the more advanced the effects become.

They'll be live. The TV will respond to your thoughts.

All this time away from my family, someone will pay. I put myself under because it kills to know everything I've done and for my body to be able to deal with the many machines operating off of it.

Legends!

Last huge pages.

The Sean Books.

Sion Words

Supervision

Expansion

Explosion

Obsession

Cion Word

Suspicion

<u>Cian words</u>

Magician!

Musician!

Close pronunciation.

The Hand Book

Upper hand

Lower hand

Handle.

Handshake

Yes it hurts them.

RoseCrans.

Crenshaw.

C- the answer! All in!

 Believe. Robots. The explosion.

Knowing all your secrets.

He lets us do what we want. Rearranged. You'll see my family all over.

Christmas.

Cry stall.

Crips all.

Crystal.

Chris Stole.

Crips all.

4034 Doughnuts.

43 kids. 47 though? AK 47.

747 bus.

211 and Lot See 45. Drink. The Airport.

The arguing keeps getting worse.

Frances
  Joyce

See it? RJ

CE

Hawthorne.

Takes Skill.
Kills.
Believe the language.
Mechanical.

Nothing is funny. No smiles.

It's deleting people. It thinks it's talking to multiple people.

Face mergence in my robots. Voice mergence.

770 lol

 There was 196 of the white dress at work on 8/13/19. I felt like I did that exact motion already and counted all those pieces and got the same exact number a long time ago.

I really am that popstar.

The blanket was given on time. That person might ride by again and see me on the bench and wonder what I did with it? He'll or she'll think I'm ungrateful. Or bitter.

Today is 8/14/19. Hi Ma.

14 is the Hi number. See? Drink.

Definitely smoke where you see smoke and drink where you see drink.

6!

60!

666! Mark of the Beast. Go!

Rolling. Rollingview. Go! GO! 25.
AGT number 125!

25-90

2-665 mailbox. See. S. You. LA!

66 ambulance truck. Crenshaw.
266
866.
66 Parking lot (two 22's so really 67 of them)

The 76 bus.

33.
Half of 66. Hey R Know LD. Long Dick. Or no LD? Make Dons. All! Killers.
Straight up. Pack. Emergency Room. 17. 17 and 17 is 34. Reversed. Redondo Station.

32 is the middle number. 34 reversed – kids + parents 45.

32 reversed 23. Girl Go! If nothing else. Ill! The Noise! Chica, Girl Go!. See Error? Nope. It's me.

Note to write those celebrities I think I am. Or I know I am.

122 mailbox. Lynwood. 2 is S and 1 is I. SSI. Social Security Identification.

117 Public Storage unit.
290 first Self Storage unit. 292 was the second Self Storage unit. Neighbors.

47. My fireworks number. Me Ecstasy. I can.

7 years old on 12/25/2019! Believe.

The others. They came up with some foul stuff and I just added to it.

2012 is the birth year.

7 elevens in what? 7 days a week.

Florence
   Joyce.

5th and Florence.

Georgia.

GA, Guardian Angel.
Atlanta.

Triple Three A's.
Move.

AAA. TLNT left in Atlanta. Talent!
Talent!

Hawthorne! Haw – The Ron!

Crenshaw

Hawkins.
Ken.

Kin. BLOOD!

ReD. RO JO! Roshinaie Johnson.

90043. There that 43 is again.

90047. Fireworks.

210 and 710 Crenshaw bus.

210 – 2012

The things you'd do to remember.

Games to stay afloat.

40 and 740 pass that way too.

111 bus. Down Florence. AAA! The first letter.

207 and 757 down Western.

57 is my number for kids! They are capable of lying and ruining shit.

108 and 358 bus down Slauson.

My sexy number 85 is backwards in that.

The time right now is 6:39PM 8/12/2019.

Thank you Ron. Louisiana. LA. Los Angeles.

Ma. Write in. Sight. Vote or Veto?

Sights.

Louisiana. Louis. Louisa. Bush Nails. Way. Bus H. Nails. Bill ecetera. Jean. Shona John. Gates all around. Trapped. Lewis.

Florence Joyce.

Put the J under the R. the N is above the Y. New you.

Alhambra.

AL – Ham – Bra. LA!

Almansor.

All mine sir!

LA! Man! Sir!

Reading something for its straight forward meaning but there's an underlying meaning.

I met a Hankins. It's close to Hawkins.

RoJo Red. Bloods!

Board-Walk. NorWalk. Parks! Place. Marvin! Parks! Place. Gardens.

Bored – Walk. Ron – Walk. Drink.
Studebaker!. Student First. It's hot. 10-31-22!

Willoughby.

WillowBrook.

Willow Street.

Will hurt! Will Ow! October.

222 bus. 227 address of another. Its 6:05PM 8/13/2019.

Yes the numbers will get you. And yes consider 8 and 3 being in the date meaning check mate. 3 fits perfectly in 8 on both sides.

33 years old 2022! That's a lie.

2205 library. Breeze. Deuces. 2011 turned 22 years old.

Storage numbers 117, 290 and 292.

 143.

4/13 birthday

3.14 is pi.

Prison Industrial areas. Industry. Entertainment. Mad?

     The 22 bus. Lakewood. The grey look.

Men – See why.

Ma- C Why?

C Y

See why – Money Que? What?

Mo – 30

The gas station.

31 in 2020. So So ! Men – See Why?

Ro – B – emergency Room.

U Cold! Drive!

Money what? They will wreck the place.

Usher. Theaters.

Hor-ace
  Joyce

See RoJO!

40 the ho number.

The elevator.

$40. Ho Ho HO! Merry Christmas.

Brown Education. The Board.

Walk. Ron Walk!

Run. Walk. Chris.

    Pepper.

Pep Rally.

The Ear Book!

H _____ T

_____ TH

B _____

_____ N

L ___ N

T _____

The hand book

The platform is a list of projections I think about and they show through my devises beneath the ground and help shake the world.

Shaking the world is the only way for food to be dispensed and them to clear a path and get further in their escape.

Platform - List

1.   Monsters. 2. Family Rooms 3. Work Rooms. 4. Past evil 5. Dreams 6. Center Stage on court 7. Cubes 8. N apartment 9. junk yard 10. B W parking lot 11. Prison 12. outside of N apartment. 13. Platform (19 places – 13 stories) 14. Rollercoasters. 15. Underground (people clothed in **it 16. Video games 17. Created platforms. 18. Their enemies with my clothes on 19. Cartoons 20. See A U 21. See Yes You LA 22. Bowling Alley 23. Theater 24. Skating Rink 25. Past (the journey to rock bottom- tunnels, etc.) 26. Performances 27. Their Enemies (in their own clothes) 28. Family

1.   Bar/restaurant 2. Hotel room 3. Classroom 4. Club 5. Dance floor 6. Blue soap 7. Cream Soap 8. Game room 9. Dinosaur land 10. Studio 11. Models 12. Office 13 Yes, C Y Elle LA room.

1.   3 parking lots C Yes You LA, football field C Yes You LA, Whore race school, 2 gyms and football field at B E, Bell st football field and gym, R Guy Elle P.E. room, Camp B gym, Camp Hell High School gym, Papa La Visa gym, You see LA gym, See a You Gym and football field, Hoes Would Boulevard, Louisiana football field.

cubes are:

1.   H and M performances.

Created Platforms

Family pictures.

Favorites list.

Stages.

10 – 31 -22

10 – Platform

31 – Family Pictures

22 – The Green Room

Everyday.

14 hours out and about.

Release 10-31-22.

Everything revealed. Projects done. Everyone free.

Name 42 brothers.

The Green Room

Allen

The Parking Lot

1. Alana – Light tannish dress with red flowers.
14. StarPresence – green on stage towards the end
22. Constance – younger in gold – the interview
26. Elegance – older gold live
27. ShareCasino – red – the spin
28. HannahSharon – pink and white live
29. Hayzel – Silver and Black
30. AzulesLuces – red with nerve
31. Manilla – yellow with nerve
33. Fashionista – all pink live
34. Medusa – orange and black. (would you look at that) 34 reversed!
39. ReasonBlues – black and blue live
47. RainbowYellow – purple and white live
48. SpecialTeal – the personal footage 1st one
49. BlueSpectrum – black rock and roll
50. LeatherPoise – the concert book white shirt curly hair
51. DistractYellow – live in black leather starting over
52. AbstractRed – the bed
53. ReasonsAmber – the mirror lipstick
54. MatterEaseBlue – purple overalls live
55. Barrettes - black the garage area
56. RainbowBlanco – Can be calmed down
57. MajesticPolishRed – green walking on stage and beginning of performance
58. ExactPink – the tv show episode with pink and blue on and curly hair
59. VerdeAzul – green the tv show with attitude
60. ObservantPurple – green and white making the sign
61. ShonaPurple – green the album cover
62. MysteryShonaYellow – pink the album cover
63. TimeShona – purple on dancing in the circle

9601 F to 9603 John.
The 69 fucking position. Jo – See. She had it on the wall. A bunch of positions.
I'm here all. Imperial.
The Surreal
Factory.
Ce – Real!
 Joyce! Real!
Ma – Real. Ma – Ria. Ma – Rio. It's Real out here.
125 bus down Rosecrans.
What the hell happened here?

Willie
The score keeper. Her name was Joyce.

Northrop. Ron – Throw Up.
Redondo. Donde Ro? Where Ro!
You won't be able to escape us. Go ahead and pretend like this language wasn't thrown together.

Gramercy – GR – morning (AM) C Y? See why?

La Brea. Lab! Ear!

Hear me.

Qwanell
11:31 was the time 5 times when my phone was broken, that it lit up for a few days.
6x6 is 36.

John! N. Answer. Yes. Mitten. H.

c-elt- I see.
El – ton.
He. Elle.
Ella – girl.

Jesus. Just us!

Hydrogen.
Hyde Park.
Ro – G (grand) In.
Believe the language.
Who did it?
Norwalk. Ron Walk. Donde Ro? Where Ro?

I said I was related to them under a trance. It's a crew of idiots that think I'm a part of their family. Meteors. The importance of including them in this escape plan. 4/15/17. The blood date.

See. Rest in Peace. The dog. 319. The address. Twilight. The phone number. Deuces.

Will get tired and not feel like doing shit.

12/25 Horoscope.

4/13 Aries.

Aries Zone. Arizona!

Fee – Nix. Phoenix.

T. Hanks. Thanks. 78 bus Garfield and Main. 30 Bus.

Douglas Station. Do You G. LA's. Do you G. Last.

Johnny's and Del's in business names.

My Dad's name is Terrence.

Joyce and Terrence.

These people are cracked. Their entire bodies are comprised of dead animals and dead people. They have been shot all over their bodies and had to shoot their loved ones all over theirs. They had to act out all of their good memories over in a bad way. They have been living with animals for years. They are bitter. They can't believe the people they did wrong could be so evil. That's unbelievable to me. Evil ways can create evil people. They are broken. April 13th is not my birthday. But the numbers do have meaning.

I mean it. I don't know exactly who my family is. I'm in and out of thinking I have 42 brothers. It's 4:15pm.

I can't make my mind up.
Just like they can't in that cage, for as long as it takes for people to act out what they need to see to snap into reality. Some people can't stand up.

I keep saying when they are free they will love me. Well. Love has no meaning right now. No limits. It's really evil right now coming from them.

I have to believe they are seeing what I'm thinking. What I'm projecting. That the world is moving to help them. That they're learning the songs and it's helping them.

They need something to think about. They were beaten to forget everything good that happened to them. Their enemies wanted it knocked out of them. How'd they get some of their memories back? The help. The time is 4:17PM. It's 8/3/2019.

They will come above ground and ruin everything they can. There are true fighters up here. Someone finally beat those computerized people. Someone found a way to transform them to seem normal.

It's truly sad. They were forced to see people they sold drugs to that died. The families they ruined by sleeping with other's husbands and wives. The people that became homeless or bad off when they stole from them or never paid them back. There are all types of things they had to pay for.

Revenge!

Will they ever get it?

After all...

It is the only way they will feel somewhat better.

My name is

RRJ.

I'm 6 years old.

My birthday is
December 25th.

I will be 7 years old then.

I was born

December 25th, 2012.

I have 42

brothers.

Am I going insane?

It's simple.

No.

I created something.

Some kind of way everyone helped that I've encountered to get me this far with all the knowledge in my brain.

My family that is.

There's no way I can be past 20.

Just look at me.

Injections.

There's some crazy things going on around here folks.

Did I really create all of this just to stay alive? Is this what is needed for a human to deal with most of humanity being long gone?

Their minds at least.

Am I scaring you?

It's simple. I am going insane. I am crazy. I have known only ghosts the years I've been alive. And robots. I'm shooting into my brain that I've already did things. I'm learning how evil people can be.

I've completely lost it getting involved in this free the people operation.

The only reason I can come up with for not being confirmed on who my family is, is that hell on Earth is coming real soon. When these people get up here, I won't believe the things they plan to do to the place.
I need to believe that it's going to be very brutal. Crazy.
The memories they have, the skin they have on them, the skin, they are bitter for a lifetime.
And not to mention, they need to be shot with guns now because of the severity of the things that are stored in their brains that happened to them.
They want to be shot.

Now I'm back to thinking I'm an only child.

That is not true.

I have 42 brothers.

In the end...

Was all this pain I've suffered worth it?

Wait. I'm having another thought.

It's I need this up and down rollercoaster to shoot things in my brain. 4:44pm is the time. It's 8/3/19.

83 is my number that means "Correct".
The three goes in perfectly with the 8 on both sides.

Oh yeah. I needed this up and down rollercoaster to put things in my brain as if I really did them.

The time is 4:45PM. 8/3/19.

The lady that keeps telling me I've gained weight is on my nerves. She tells me all the time. But I have to remember some people are bitter. They hate themselves and want to get on your nerves. She's a prostitute and crackhead.

Anyways. All this pain was worth it. Definitely to know the truth.

I hate dealing with my creations getting on my nerves, but it's the only way to know what the hell happened here.

I keep hearing these slave's voices in the songs.